Simon and Marshall's Excellent Adventure

It was on my paper route that I first noticed something strange. Someone was following me, and he was picking up the newspapers I had thrown. I couldn't believe it. Somebody was stealing the papers I was delivering!

All I could see was that the thief was about my size and age, with blond hair and the weirdest backpack I've ever seen. It was all silver and glittery. And he was riding a bicycle that didn't have any wheels. I don't mean that the wheels had been stolen, but that it didn't seem to *need* them. It just seemed to float in the air, about the same distance off the ground as if there had been wheels there.

I have to admit that, in all my time in Eerie, I'd never seen anything like this before . . .

Simon and Marshall's Excellent Adventure

John Peel

MACMILLAN CHILDREN'S BOOKS

First published 1997 by Avon Books, USA
a division of The Hearst Corporation

This edition published 1999 by Macmillan Children's Books
a division of Macmillan Publishers Limited
25 Eccleston Place, London SW1W 9NF
Basingstoke and Oxford

Associated companies throughout the world

ISBN 0 330 37070 7

1 3 5 7 9 8 6 4 2

A CIP catalogue record for this book is available
from the British Library

Printed and bound in Great Britain by Mackays of Chatham plc, Kent

PROLOGUE

My name is Marshall Teller. Not too long ago, I was living in New Jersey, just across the river from New York City. It was crowded, polluted, and full of crime. I loved it. But my parents wanted a better life for my sister and me. So we moved to a place so wholesome, so squeaky clean, so ordinary that you could only find it on TV— Eerie, Indiana.

It's the American Dream come true, right? Wrong. Sure, my new hometown *looks* normal enough. But look again. Underneath, it's crawling with strange stuff. Item: Elvis lives on my paper route. Item: Bigfoot eats out of my trash. Item: I see unexplained flashing lights in the sky at least once a week. No one believes me, but Eerie is the center of weirdness for the entire planet.

And now, I'm getting so used to the freakiness, weird things don't even surprise me as much as they used to. I mean, at one time, I would have thought that it was impossible for people to make themselves invisible. But now . . . I'm not so sure. In fact, I have reason to believe that an invisible boy has been stealing my chewed gum. Now that might sound paranoid to most people.

But not to my friend Simon Holmes. Simon's my next-door neighbor. He's lived in Eerie his whole life, and he's the only other person who knows just how freaky this place is. Together, we've been keeping a record of all the stuff that happens around here. We've faced some of Eerie's most bizarre inhabitants and lived to tell about it, from the talking dogs that tried to take over the city to the crazy gray-haired kid who lives in the old abandoned mill and can't remember who he is. I told you this place was weird.

Still don't believe me? You will.

1

*T*he weirdness started when I was getting ready to go on my paper route. I don't like to leave the house unless I'm wearing my favorite sneakers. They're old and kind of battered, but they fit my feet perfectly. And that morning they weren't where I'd left them, next to my bed.

Mom had bought me a brand-new pair two weeks earlier. They were okay, but needed some serious wearing in. I figured that my missing sneakers were Mom's way of telling me to accelerate the wearing-in program.

"Have you seen my old sneakers?" I asked her when I went downstairs.

"Not since yesterday," Mom answered cheerfully. "When you were still wearing them. Aren't you ever going to use that nice new pair I bought you?"

3

I turned to my older sister Syndi. "Did you move them?"

"As if I'd touch your ratty old sneakers," she said with a sniff. "You probably just lost them."

"I never lose things," I told her. I went to look for the new sneakers that Mom had bought me. Actually, they were pretty cool. Just a little tight in places. And they were still stiff and shiny. Well, I'd have to get used to them. Leaving the house, I jumped on my bike and went to collect my papers.

Having a paper route is a great way to make money and keep an eye on the neighborhood at the same time. And in my neighborhood there's always something going on. I cycled along my route, tossing newspapers onto everyone's front walk as I rode. As usual, a middle-aged man in a rhinestone-studded bathrobe came out immediately to get his.

"Thank you," he called. "Thank you very much." He spoke in a low musical voice.

"You're welcome!" I called, glancing back. He was already on his way into the house for his breakfast of fried banana sandwiches. Even out here I could smell them cooking.

And that's when I noticed something strange.

Someone was following me, and he was picking up one of the newspapers I had thrown. He tossed it into some kind of basket, and then started to move on to the next paper.

I couldn't believe it. Somebody was stealing the papers I was delivering!

"Hey!" I yelled. "What do you think you're doing?" I started pedaling furiously toward the thief. I was too far away to make out his face or anything. All I could see was that he was about my size and age, with blond hair and the weirdest backpack I've ever seen. It was all silver and glittery.

And he was riding a bicycle that didn't have any wheels. I don't mean that the wheels had been stolen or anything, but that it didn't seem to *need* them. It just seemed to float in the air, about the same distance off the ground as if there had been wheels there. The basket behind him was floating in the air, too. And it wasn't attached to him or the bike by anything.

I have to admit that, in all my time in Eerie, I'd never seen anything like this before.

"What do you think you're doing?" I called out again.

The thief looked up and realized he'd been spotted. Immediately he whirled the bike around and sped away at least three times faster than I could go on my bike. The basket followed along behind him in the air, like a dog running after its owner on a walk.

I didn't bother trying to chase the kid. Instead, I checked to see how many papers he'd stolen. It looked like he'd only grabbed four, but he was clearly after more. Luckily, I was near the end of my route at this point, so I finished it and reported the theft of the four papers to my boss. He promised to call Sergeant Knight at the police station and report it. Then he gave me four papers, and I redelivered them.

But I was puzzled. Why would anyone want to steal four copies of the same paper? I mean, he could hardly be making a profit selling them. And if he just wanted to read one, he would have taken just one.

And then there was his crazy bike. It obviously had to have some kind of motor in it, but it hadn't made any noise. It might have been some kind of new invention I'd never heard of before, but I seriously doubted it. Wouldn't something like that be all over the news?

So . . . what was it? As usual, I didn't have a clue—yet.

On the bus to school, I told Simon all about it

and we agreed that we should look into the situation. Simon's pretty neat, for a younger kid. He's very smart, and he's got lots of guts. We make a great investigative team. His eyes widened as I told him about the thief. "Neat!"

"Yeah." I shook my head. "I wish I'd managed to get a better look at him. It could have been any blond-haired kid from my grade."

"Well, at least you scared him off," Simon said.

"Maybe." I wasn't so sure about that. "But this is Eerie, don't forget. You can't scare off weirdness just by yelling at it. At least, it's never worked that way before."

I was sure that I'd be seeing more of the thief pretty soon. Since Simon was two grades below me, we went to our separate classes agreeing to meet up for lunch.

In homeroom, my teacher, Mr. Dupries, gave the usual announcements, ending with the fact that Mayor Culpa would be speaking at a special assembly for the whole school the following Monday morning, and we should all at least try to look presentable for it. Then he smiled at us, which usually meant bad news.

"And we have a new student with us for a while," he said brightly. He waved his hand toward a new kid sitting at the front of the class. "This is Jazen Karter, class. I hope you'll all be very friendly, and show him what a nice town this is. He's staying here temporarily with his grandfather, Mr. Foreman."

Jazen looked around and smiled shyly at the class. He was blond-haired, and about the build of the thief I'd chased earlier. Was it possible that *he* was my thief? I didn't smile back. I decided that it might be smart to keep an eye on him.

On the way to our first class I introduced myself. "Marshall Teller," I told him, sticking out my hand. He just stared at it, as if nobody had ever offered to shake hands with him before and it was a custom he'd never even heard of. Well, it takes all kinds, so I let my hand fall. "Welcome to Eerie."

"Thanks, Marshall," he said, blushing slightly. Could it be guilt? I'd find out soon enough. "Seems like a nice town."

"Yeah. It *seems* like one," I agreed. Jazen looked fairly normal, but there was something odd about him I couldn't quite pin down. Then it clicked. He was wearing a Grateful Dead T-shirt. But his was spelled "Great Full Dead." Maybe it was some kind of a joke—I couldn't tell, but it definitely added to his weirdness factor. "So, how long are you stuck here for?" I asked.

"I'm not quite sure," he replied. "It depends."

"On what?"

He shrugged. "Things."

Well, you couldn't argue with *that,* could you?

I tried to get some more information out of him, but he didn't exactly open up. Oh, he was willing to talk, but he didn't actually say a lot. For example, when I asked him where his grandfather lived, he just said: "East of town a bit." That's the kind of thing he did. Nothing rude, just never quite answering the question.

Okay, I'd try again later. Maybe he was just shy, or maybe he didn't like being around me. If he'd been the one stealing my papers, I might be making him pretty nervous. When we reached our class, he settled down at the back, about five seats behind me. When Miss Weston, the math teacher, arrived, I took out the gum I'd been chewing and put it in its old wrapper in the corner of my desk.

Math is math, and I'm okay at it, I guess. But I can't really get enthusiastic about it. Maybe it's not meant to be an endurance test to stick it out to the end of the period, but it sure feels like it. Eventually, though, the bell rang, and class was over. I packed my books and slipped my homework into my notebook. I'd managed a B plus, which was pretty good. Then I reached for my gum.

It was gone.

My first thought was that it had fallen to the floor. I bent down and peered under the desk, but there was no gum.

This was getting to be majorly weird now. How could my gum have disappeared from my desk while I was sitting at it?

I glanced back, but Jazen was still in his seat. I couldn't figure this one out, so I decided to move on, instead. I picked up my notebook, and then realized that my corrected homework wasn't in it anymore.

Somehow, it had been stolen while I was looking under the desk for my gum.

2

When I told Simon at lunch about what had happened, he couldn't believe it. "Stolen while you were there, and you didn't see anything?" he asked.

"Nothing," I admitted. "Even when Al and Lodgepoole take something, you can see them if you're watching. Whoever's after me is way ahead of them in technique." Al and Lodgepool worked at Eerie's Bureau of Lost and were responsible for unmatching a lot of the socks in Eerie. They kept all the odds and ends that they found in a huge underground tunnel system. But they weren't very smooth at what they did. And they weren't quick enough to steal the gum right out from under my nose.

"So what are we going to do?" Simon asked.

"I don't like being victimized," I told him. "I'm

going to find out whoever's doing this to me, and stop him."

"I'm with you," Simon promised, his eyes sparkling at the thought of another mystery. "Hey! He's struck again!"

I followed Simon's gaze. The straw had vanished from my juice while we'd been talking. And neither of us had seen anyone even close to our table. I glanced around, and saw that Jazen was sitting by himself three tables away, apparently intent on analyzing his burger. I couldn't blame him. I've often wondered what they put in them myself.

"The weird new kid," Simon remarked. "Is he the chief suspect?"

"So far, he's the only suspect," I admitted. "The problem is, if it *is* him, I can't see how he can be doing this. He didn't come near our table at all."

Simon nodded. "And the stuff that's being taken is kind of strange," he pointed out. "Four newspapers, a stick of used gum, and a straw. Whoever's doing this can't be doing it for the money."

"Maybe they're just doing it to bug me," I grumbled. "But I think we can use that to our advantage."

After school, Simon and I went to my house and up to the attic. The attic is where we keep our Evidence Locker, in which we stash all our notes and small objects that reveal how weird Eerie is. I was hoping to find a clue to my missing belongings among all the records we'd kept. But nothing. Then I had an idea. I told Simon my plan.

"It's the old noose-in-the-grass trick," I explained to Simon. "I'm going to finish that model kit of the stealth jet I've been working on, and then leave it out in the yard right next to the trap. When the thief goes for it, we pull on the noose and get him."

"Excellent." Simon approved.

So we set up the noose trap first, covering it carefully with grass and leading the rope from it behind a tree large enough to hide me. Simon would take up his position on the deck, and watch the model plane. When he saw someone go for it, he'd signal me, and then I'd pull the rope. Simple, but the best plans often are.

So, of course, are the worst.

I finished the model, and then placed it in the grass, right in the center of the noose. Then we hid and waited. I'd expected that it would be ages before our mysterious thief took the bait, but I was amazed. It was less than two minutes before Simon waved to me.

I jerked on the rope, and then leaped out into the open.

Nothing.

The rope was just lying there on the grass, and the model had disappeared. Simon came to me, his mouth hanging open.

"I didn't see anything," he told me. "The plane just rose into the air, and I signaled you. And then the plane vanished, and you pulled on the rope."

"Bizarre," I agreed, realizing the noose wasn't about to trap someone we couldn't see. "The way I figure it, there are two choices. Either I'm being stalked by an invisible man or by a ghost."

Before coming to Eerie, I would never have considered either of these possibilities. But I'd already met three ghosts in Eerie and I figured that anything was possible. "But why would a ghost be interested in a model airplane?" I wondered aloud.

"Or even a newspaper," Simon added. "After all, dead people aren't very interested in current affairs."

"True. So I guess that means I'm being stalked by an invisible man."

"If that's possible," Simon said.

14

"In Eerie," I informed him, "*anything* is possible. The more impossible it seems, the more likely it is."

"Okay, so let's say it *is* an invisible man," Simon conceded. "How would we catch him?"

I thought about this for a few minutes.

"We have to find a way to make him visible," I said. "We could spread dust over the floors in the house so that his footprints would show up when he walked."

"Cool," Simon agreed. "But your Mom might be upset. And doing it outside wouldn't be much use, since the wind would blow it away."

"True enough," I agreed. "So let's go with plan B."

My Dad's a total pack rat, and hates throwing anything away. So I knew we'd find all the equipment we needed in the garage. Sure enough, we turned up two cans of spray paint, which were almost completely full.

"Time for another trap," I told Simon. "Only this time, we'll both hide on the deck, and leave the bait close to the edge of the lawn, where we can see it. Then, when the thief strikes, we leap up and spray the area. The paint will hit him and then we'll be able to grab him."

I fetched an old pair of socks from my room, and "accidentally" dropped them on the grass, close to the edge of the deck. Simon and I pretended to go in, but instead we crept back on our hands and knees and hid behind two large planters.

Once again, the thief struck far faster than I'd expected. Simon and I had hardly gotten to our places before the socks began to float up into the air.

Simon and I leaped up and sprayed in the direction of the socks. "Stop, thief!" I called out at the top of my lungs.

What *should* have happened was that the paint would stick to the invisible man, and we'd see the shape of his body. What *did* happen was the exact opposite. The paint simply vanished when it got close to where the thief was carrying away the socks.

Then, out of thin air, there was a sneeze, and we both automatically said "Bless you!" before realizing where it had come from. Simon and I vaulted off the deck, grabbing at the air.

We came up with exactly nothing.

The invisible thief had stolen my socks and made his getaway again. The paint idea had been a washout.

It was time for extra heavy thinking, and that meant a trip to World of Stuff, where we could get some burgers and ice-cream sundaes. Food usually helped us think. Maybe chocolate is brain food, or something. But today it just wasn't working.

"Is everything okay, boys?" asked Mr. Radford. His moustache wiggled as he grinned down at us. "You're looking unusually serious today."

We don't really like to confide in the adults in Eerie. Whatever weirdness there is in the town seems to affect the older people the most. Sometimes other kids notice the strange things that go on, but the adults never even realize that there's anything wrong at all.

Of course, Mr. Radford's not like other adults. He would have to be put in a category all his own. And sometimes he does manage to help us out.

So I told him. "I'm being stalked by an invisible thief who's snatching all my stuff."

He sat down at the table with us, his nose twitching. "Hmmm. I can see how that could be a problem. I imagine you've tried to catch him?"

"Twice," I replied. "And he got away both times."

"We tried spraying him with paint," Simon added. "But the paint just turned invisible, too."

"Shame," Mr. Radford said. "That sounds like a good idea." He thought for a moment. "But you know what your problem is, boys? You're too honest."

"What do you mean?" I asked.

"There's an old saying, 'Set a thief to catch a thief.'"

I had to admit that it wasn't a bad idea.

Simon looked confused, so I explained. "What Mr. Radford means is that we're honest people, and we can't outsmart a crook who's this sneaky. So what we need to do is to find another crook who's even sneakier, and get him to help us."

There was only one person sneaky enough to fit the bill and we both thought of him at the same instant.

"Dash!" we both exclaimed.

Dash is one of the strangest characters in Eerie, and that's saying a lot, all things considered. He'd wandered into town one day, with no idea of who he was or what he was doing here. He looked, mostly, like a teenage boy, except for the fact that he had the gray hair of a sixty-year-old man. Not only couldn't he remember where he came from or why, he didn't even know his real name.

To say that Simon and I had very mixed

feelings about Dash would be putting it [...]
Dash could be okay at times, but mostly he[...]
trouble. Dash could be really mean, and he was a
petty criminal. Mr. Radford had banned him from
World of Stuff because of his shoplifting problem.

But in this case, I realized that Dash could be
the one person who would be able to help us out.
He had one of the sneakiest minds I'd ever
known, and I felt sure he could think circles
around our thief.

If we could get him interested in helping out.

Dash didn't live in Eerie itself. It was said that
he'd taken over an old shack in the woods outside
of town, where he lived by himself. He didn't trust
other people any more than they trusted him, so he
never told anyone exactly where he lived. I hoped
that wouldn't turn out to be too much of a problem.

It was a nice day, and the woods were sort of
okay. Simon and I headed in the direction where
we thought Dash was living. On the way, a foot-
long fish with what looked like a cross between
flippers and legs darted across our path and into
the bushes. It would have been a cool trophy to
grab, but carrying around a fish all afternoon
didn't sound like a very sanitary concept, so we
were forced to ignore it. A few minutes later, we

passed a dodo that just sat there and watched us. These birds didn't seem to be bothered by people, even though they were often caught and eaten. Talk about slow learners!

And then, finally, there was movement in the bushes, and Dash stepped out into the path. He was dressed in his usual loose-fitting raincoat and wore his usual don't-mess-with-me look. "Okay," he growled. "That's far enough for your nature ramble. Time to go home."

"Actually," I told him. "We were looking for you."

"I didn't do it," he said promptly. "Whatever it was, I deny it categorically. I wasn't even there at the time, no matter what anyone says."

"Relax," I told him. "We just want your help."

"*Relax,* you say," he grumbled. "After half-scaring me to death? And now you say you want my help?" He looked thoughtful. "What's in it for me?"

"The knowledge that you're helping a friend in trouble?" Simon said meekly.

Dash sneered. "I don't have any friends, short stuff. And if I were going to look for some, you two wouldn't be candidates."

Trying to appeal to his better nature obviously

wasn't working. He didn't have one. So I decided to appeal to a part of him that I knew was well developed: his greed. "How about a fifty-fifty split of the reward?" I offered.

"Seventy-five, twenty-five," he countered. "In *my* favor."

"What makes you think we need your help that much?" I asked him.

"The fact that you're here looking for me," he answered cheerfully.

I pretended to think it over. Since I wasn't actually sure there was going to be any reward at all, I was hardly losing anything by agreeing. "Okay," I finally said. Then I explained the problem, and told Dash about our first two attempts to capture the invisible thief.

"Tricky," Dash admitted.

"So you can't help?" asked Simon.

"I didn't say that," Dash countered.

"You're the sneakiest person in Eerie," I told him. "If you can't catch this guy, nobody can."

"Thanks," Dash replied. "But I'm actually the sneakiest person on Earth. This bozo doesn't stand a chance against me. So let's get to work."

Well, so far we were doing pretty well. We'd managed to intrigue Dash enough to get him to agree to help us. And if *he* couldn't catch our thief, then I knew nobody could.

And his help would be coming just in time. When I got home again, one of the sheets had vanished from my bed, along with an old T-shirt. This was getting serious, and it was definitely time to put a stop to it.

3

"You know what your problem is?" Dash said to me as he worked on his trap.

"You, most of the time," I replied.

"Yeah, I guess so," he admitted. "But I meant in this instance. Your problem is that you're too nice."

I couldn't help smiling at that. "Well, that's one thing nobody could ever accuse you of being."

"True," he agreed. "And that means I'm much more likely to succeed in what I attempt than you are. I don't worry about minor points, like ethics."

I wasn't too sure I liked the direction that this conversation was taking. "Let's get something straight," I said. "You *are* setting a trap to catch this guy, not to kill him or anything, right?"

"Yeah, sure," Dash said, rolling his eyes. "He'll definitely be alive when he's caught. But I won't promise he won't be a little frayed around the edges, okay? Or will that upset your delicate stomach?"

"He's only stolen some old junk from me," I insisted. "Nothing valuable. I don't think that's grounds for hurting him."

"There, you see?" Dash asked, pointing a screwdriver at me. "That's your problem, right there. You've got *victim* written all over you, and it's in your own handwriting. If this guy's ripping you off, you've got to make certain he learns the error of his ways. Roughing him up a bit will do that."

I didn't much like his line of reasoning. "So, how does this trap of yours work?" I asked him.

"Really simple," Dash answered, holding up a small switch he'd just finished putting together. "Your traps were too obvious, and this thief got around them. I'm going for the no-strings-attached concept. What's keeping Simon?"

"He'll be here any second," I said. I'd sent him up to my room for an old basketball from my closet.

Right on cue, Simon came running out of the house. "He struck again," he announced. "Inside the house, this time. Two of your books vanished from your desk while I was getting the basketball."

"Books?" Dash shook his head. "This crook must be mental. He's got some way of stealing stuff while he's invisible, and all he does is steal junk." He glared at me. "And from you, of all people. If *I* had invisibility, I'd put it to better use."

"Stealing much more valuable things, I imagine," I replied.

"Sure," said Dash. "There's lots of cash in the banks, and jewelry and stuff. Trust me, that's what I'd go for. Why this guy is wasting his time on you, I'll never know."

"Maybe you will," I pointed out. "If we can catch him."

"No *problemo*," Dash declared. He took the ball and went over to the tree he'd been preparing. He carefully placed the switch under the ball, and then we all walked back to the deck.

"So," Simon said, "how does this brilliant trap of yours work?"

"Sheer genius," Dash answered. "When the thief picks up the ball, it will make the switch click. No wires or anything around to alert him to trouble. He won't think of looking up."

A large packing case was suspended from one of the thickest branches of the tree. Dash had fixed a metal strip to the top of it. Then he'd hooked up an electromagnet and fixed it to the tree.

"I get it," I said. "The switch sends a pulse to the electromagnet above him, which turns off."

"And drops the crate over his head," Dash finished. "You may applaud my genius any time you're ready. Now would be good," he added, far from modestly.

"I hate to admit it," I told him, "but it does sound like a good idea."

"The best," Dash assured me. We were all sitting on the deck, sipping some of Mom's fresh lemonade, and pretending not to watch the ball at all. We had our backs to it, but Dash had set up a pocket mirror on the table so we could see if anything happened.

I'll give our thief one thing—he didn't believe in wasting time. We'd barely finished half of our lemonade when the ball suddenly jerked up into the air.

The switch gave a little jump and clicked loudly enough so that even we could hear it. Then the packing case came hurtling down from the branch and hit the ground with a *whuump*.

We were on our feet and rushing across the lawn toward it in seconds.

But whatever we'd caught got mad. There was a crash, and the side of the crate cracked open. Another punch, and the opening widened. Then an invisible fist punched a third hole in the side of the crate, and now the hole was big enough to let out whoever, or whatever, had been trapped inside.

"You're not getting away!" Dash yelled, and threw himself at the opening in the crate. He landed on *something,* even though none of us could see what it was. It was really weird, seeing Dash holding onto something invisible, suspended a foot or so off the ground. "Yikes!" he howled. "It's strong!"

Just how strong became apparent when Dash suddenly went flying into the bushes with a yelp. Simon and I looked at each other and jumped for the invisible thing. We were in between it and freedom, and not about to let it get away. Well, that was the idea, anyway.

The invisible thing had other plans. It had dropped the basketball and pushed forward. Simon and I were ready, and although I couldn't see anything, I could definitely feel something. It felt like a human arm, so I grabbed hold, hard and fast. Simon seemed to have grabbed onto his other arm.

But our invisible guy didn't even slow down. He just raised both arms, and we discovered that we were floating about three feet from the ground, held up by nothing at all. It didn't feel good, but it felt marvelous compared to what happened next.

The invisible thief shook both arms really hard. My jaws rattled and knocked together. It was impossible to keep hold of him, and a moment later I hit the ground hard, managing to land on my hands and knees.

Meanwhile, Dash had recovered enough to throw himself on the invisible figure again. He must have landed on the guy's back and wrapped his arms around him. I was kind of dazed from hitting the ground, but I saw the invisible thing stop and drag Dash off his back. He must have had a hand around Dash's neck, because Dash's face went all red and he started choking. His feet kicked out, but they were a good foot off the ground, so it did no good. I was trying to get to my feet when Dash was tossed aside.

The invisible thief was gone.

Simon and I ran over to Dash, who was gasping for breath.

"You okay?" Simon asked anxiously.

"Sure." Dash gasped, his voice gravelly. "I just

love being strangled by invisible monsters. I try to do it at least once a day. You bozo! Do I *sound* okay?"

"No," I answered him. "You sound obnoxious, so you must be feeling better. And so much for your brilliant plan. This thief is obviously too smart for you, too."

"What?" Dash sat up, utterly indignant. "No way am I giving up. He may have won the first round, but the game's not over yet. I'll come up with a better trap, that's all."

"Yeah, but maybe you should think about it overnight," I said. "It's getting kind of late now, and Simon and I have homework to do."

"That's because you're chumps and go to school," Dash answered. "I never have homework to do."

Simon shook his head. "And you'll never go to college or make anything of your life, either," he pointed out.

"For all you know, pip-squeak," Dash growled, "I already did all of that. Once I get my memory back, I'll know. Till then, nobody makes me do anything I don't want to do." He nodded at us. "See you after school tomorrow. Unless you want to be smart and play hooky."

"I think I'd better play it smart and go to school," I answered.

"Suit yourself, sucker," Dash replied, and wandered away.

Simon went home for dinner, so I was left with my family for the evening.

I guess as families go, they aren't bad. Dad's kind of a space cadet, but he really enjoys his work, and there's no doubt he loves Mom, Syndi, and me. Mom tries really hard, and she has a lot of work, not only raising me and Syndi, but running her store in the mall. So, of course, a few things have to give. Like meals, for example. Mom can burn anything on Earth, even ice cream. Her recipes hardly ever work out the way they're supposed to—and that's *before* you figure in the Eerie weirdness factor. So, a lot of times I don't know exactly what it is we're eating for dinner. And believe me, when that happens, I don't ask.

Today's dinner was something brown and green. I think there was meat and broccoli in it, but I could have been wrong. It didn't taste too bad, and I had seconds. Then I took a red brownie for dessert, and headed for my room.

I noticed right away that some more things had disappeared, but nothing important. A packet of paper clips, a couple of old photos, and my old Metallica poster. My thief was getting itchy fingers, obviously. I set the brownie down and started on my homework.

Naturally, when I looked for it, the brownie had disappeared too. This was getting beyond irritating. Even my food was getting stolen, now. And I couldn't see or hear anything unusual. The thief might be standing in my room right now, watching me, planning his next move. That was a spooky thought. I considered spilling talcum powder all over the floor so I could see if there were any footprints, but I reluctantly decided not to do it. Mom would never understand.

I went out and cleaned up the wrecked case in the yard, and returned the basketball to my closet. With the door to the closet closed and me in the room, even if the thief was watching, he couldn't go for it. But I couldn't spend the rest of my life putting stuff in my closet and locking it up. I *had* to catch this crook.

At bedtime I still didn't know whether the thief was with me or not. As I brushed my teeth, something occurred to me. I was only assuming that the thief was a guy. Maybe it was a girl instead. Plenty of girls had short-cut blond hair. It was bad enough thinking I might be being watching by a guy, but the thought of an invisible girl watching me get ready for bed was more than I could stand. I decided to change in the bathroom with the door closed.

Then I went back to my room and settled into bed.

"If you're still here," I said to nobody in particular, "this is where it gets boring, because I'm going to sleep." I turned off the light and lay down.

Would anything of mine still be there when I woke up in the morning?

To my surprise, when I got ready for my paper route the next day, I didn't see any evidence that anything else had been taken. As I delivered the papers, I kept one eye on my rearview mirrors, but today the papers stayed put. There was no sign at all of the guy or girl with the odd bike. Maybe the thief was sleeping late, exhausted from his activities of the day before. I could only hope so.

At school, things were relatively quiet to begin with. An old postcard of Disney World I had taped inside my locker had disappeared, but that was all.

Jazen was back, but he was no more sociable

than he had been the day before. The kids at my school are fairly regular in at least some ways. A couple of them had tried talking to Jazen and making friends with him. Jazen was polite, but distant. He didn't seem to be interested in making friends at all. Well, Mr. Dupries had said that he was only in town for a while. And Jazen had been very vague about how long it would be when I'd talked to him. Maybe he didn't think it was worth getting to know anyone.

But I thought it might be worthwhile getting to know him. So I deliberately sat next to him in class and tried to talk.

That was when I noticed something else offbeat about Jazen. When anyone else talked to him, he seemed kind of bored, even when Jennifer Grelski talked to him—and Jeni is definitely the prettiest girl in the class, if not the school. Usually when she talks to people they feel blessed. She's okay, though, and not at all stuck-up about being drop-dead gorgeous. She even talks to me from time to time. But when she tried to talk to Jazen he just gave her his usual bored look and one-word answers until she gave up and went away.

But when I talked to him, Jazen was totally different. He seemed to be kind of embarrassed.

His face would flush and he'd chatter nervously, as if he couldn't stop. I couldn't help finding this strange, all things considered. Why talk to me, and nobody else?

Not that he actually said very much. Just jabbered nonsensically for the most part.

And today he had on another weird T-shirt. This one was of the San Diego Zoo. Except that it was spelled "Zuu," and there were two animals on it I'd never even seen before. One of them looked like a cross between a camel and a bear, only it was covered in green fur. The other was tall and spindly, like a lobster with extra long legs. I wasn't the best student of biology in the world, but I was pretty certain that nothing like those two creatures were in the San Diego Zoo.

Was this another joke T-shirt? It was possible, I guessed. Maybe Jazen just had a wacky sense of humor. But—this being Eerie—maybe there was another explanation that wasn't so normal. . . .

"Maybe he's from some weird, parallel universe where those things do exist," Simon suggested when I told him about this at lunchtime.

"It's a thought," I agreed seriously, watching to make sure my straw didn't disappear before I was done with it. I noticed that some of my fries had

34

disappeared, but that may not have been the thief; Simon had a habit of sneaking them when I wasn't looking. "Anyway, I think today we take some positive action."

"Like what?" asked Simon.

"We follow Jazen home and check him out," I replied.

"Cool," Simon agreed.

I lost a set of notes I'd taken, and had to ask for another copy of a homework assignment when I found that mine was missing. Other than that, it was a pretty normal day. As soon as the final bell rang, I hurried to find Simon. Then we got ready to follow Jazen home.

He'd told me that he lived east of town, so we hurried ahead of him in order to hide until he passed us. That way, if he suspected he was being followed, he'd never guess that it was me or Simon.

We were hiding behind the trash Dumpster at one of the strip malls on the edge of town. Some-one came by and dropped a stuffed swordfish into the bin, which Simon thought warranted a closer look. Just as he was reaching for it, we saw Jazen.

He didn't seem to see us as we fell in behind him. Simon and I kept back as far as we could, just in case Jazen turned around. But he never did. He walked down Main Street, and then toward a building site on the edge of town. This had a tall wooden fence around it, and we'd never actually seen any work being done there. There was a sign on the gate that read: MAJOR NEW SHOPPING CENTER COMING SPRING '97. Except '97 had been crossed out, and '98, and then '99, written over it. Changing the date was about all the work we'd ever seen done there.

Jazen opened the gate and went inside.

Simon and I looked at each other in confusion. What was Jazen doing on an abandoned building site? Maybe he just liked to play there on his way home, but somehow that seemed far too normal a thing for Jazen to be doing. We went up to the gate and peered around the edge. I couldn't help wondering if he'd seen us following him, and that this was a trap he'd set. Maybe he was going to jump out at us and yell boo, or something.

But nothing of the kind happened. Actually, nothing of *any* kind happened. The site was empty.

There was the fence all the way around, but no other exit. There was no construction machinery, or any sign of work being done. There was exactly one thing inside the fence, and that was one of those bright blue Porta-Johns you see on construction sites for the workers. And that didn't make any sense, either. If there were no workers, why was there a portable toilet?

The ground was completely bare: no sign of any excavation for foundations, and not a blade of grass or a weed in sight. That, too, was weird. This place hadn't been worked on in three years. It should have been overgrown, but it wasn't.

In short, there was only one possible place where Jazen could have gone, and that was into the Porta-John. Simon and I just looked at each other.

"Maybe he had to go really bad," he suggested.

"It's possible," I agreed. "Then he'll be coming out soon." We hid behind the blue box and waited. But nothing happened. After ten minutes, my patience was running thin, so I went around to the front and opened the door.

It was empty.

Simon and I couldn't figure this out. We had *seen* him enter the yard, and we had definitely *not* seen him leave. And there was nowhere for him to hide. What was going on?

"He's turned invisible," Simon declared. "That means he must be our thief."

"Maybe," I said. "Or maybe he's got a sneaky way out of here, and he just lured us over to give us the slip, for some reason." I shrugged. "I guess we'd better go home and see what Dash has cooked up today."

As we were leaving the yard, I closed the gate behind me. I glanced at the notice again and stiffened. "Simon," I said. "Look."

The sign had the words FOREMAN CON-STRUCTION printed at the top.

"Jazen said his grandfather's name was Foreman," I said. "This *is* the right place. But what happened to him?"

4

We went to my house, puzzled by what we'd seen. Or, rather, by what we *hadn't* seen. Jazen had entered an almost empty yard and simply disappeared. It certainly seemed that he had to be our invisible thief. But if he was, then why was he doing it? And how?

Maybe, if we caught him in the act, we'd find out.

Dash was waiting on the front porch, a big sneer on his face. "This one's guaranteed to floor the sucker," he assured us. He led us out into the yard, where the basketball was once more set up as bait.

"He's probably going to expect the old radio-controlled switch trick again, like yesterday," Dash said proudly. "So I've done something different this time." He gestured to the nearby tree. "Motion detectors."

Simon gave a snort. "If he's invisible, they won't detect him," he pointed out.

"I know that," Dash said smugly. "But they *will* detect the ball moving when he picks it up."

"And then what?" I asked, impressed with the first part of the plan.

"Then the log I've got suspended in the tree up there swings down like a pendulum and knocks the jerk into the middle of next week," Dash answered.

I was appalled. "Dash," I pointed out, "we want to *catch* the guy, not kill him. You could do some serious damage to him if you hit him with a log."

Dash shook his head. "Didn't you feel how strong he is?" he argued. "He lifted the two of you up off the ground. Nothing short of smacking him with a heavy log is going to make an impact on this guy. Trust me—have I ever steered you wrong?"

"Just about every time I've met you," I answered.

"But that was in the past," Dash said. "Not recently. And we're working together on this one, so why should I lie to you?"

"You need reasons to lie?" Simon asked innocently.

"Smart-mouthed kid," muttered Dash. "Look,

do you want to catch the thief or don't you? If the answer is yes, then let me do what I think is necessary, okay?"

I still wasn't completely convinced, but Dash was right in one way. Whoever this thief was, he was no ordinary person. Not only was he invisible, but he was also super strong. Maybe it *would* take a log in the breadbasket to make him stop. I was walking toward the ball, still struggling with my conscience. Then the whole issue became moot, because Simon gave a yell and pointed.

The basketball was levitating above the lawn. The motion detector lit up red, and then there was a tremendous *whoosh* as a six-foot-long log on two thick ropes swung out of the tree toward the hovering ball.

And the log didn't stop. It swung clean through, knocking the basketball to one side. And then it swung, out of control, up into the far side of the tree.

"Uh-oh," I muttered, having a bad feeling about this. All three of us ground to a halt as we realized that somehow the log had missed its intended victim.

And that it had reached the end of its swing, and was coming back down again.

Right at us.

We all dove to the ground and to one side. The log whistled past me, barely six inches over my tensed body. As soon as it *whooshed* by, I rolled out of its path. Simon and Dash had both managed to avoid being hit, and we sat in the grass, watching the log swing back and forth in the air until it came to a rest.

Suddenly we heard the sound of high-pitched laughter.

Dash's face turned red with anger. "That does it," he growled. "This time it's personal. I'm going to fix that sucker for certain with my next trap."

"How did he get out of this one?" Simon asked. He fetched the basketball. "We saw the ball rise, and then the log hit it. How come it didn't hit the thief?"

I remembered the missing gum from my desk. "Because this guy's got more gadgets up his high-tech sleeve than James Bond," I said. "Maybe he has a tractor beam that can lift things up without his having to touch them. Maybe that's how he lifted the ball."

"He knew it was a trap all along," Dash growled. "But how?"

"Well, after the trap you set yesterday, he'd have to be pretty dumb not to know," I pointed out.

"Besides," Simon added logically, "he's invisible. He could have stood right next to you while you were setting up the trap, and you wouldn't even have known."

"Good point, squirt," Dash agreed, thinking hard. He leaned forward and began to whisper. "So here's what I want you two to do tomorrow. Go somewhere very conspicuous after school with something he's likely to be interested in, and make sure he follows you. Keep him away from this house until at least six o'clock, and then come back. By that time, I'll have my next trap ready. And this is one he won't escape. You have my personal guarantee on that."

Dash was taking it badly. He really valued his title as sneakiest person in Eerie, and this invisible guy was doing serious damage to his ego. I just hoped that Dash wouldn't go too far with his next trap. Using Dash to help you was kind of like unleashing a primal force: You might get the job done, but you might just take half of Eerie with you while you were at it.

The rest of the evening was kind of nerve-racking. My fork disappeared while I was eating dinner. Again, I wasn't sure what the food was, but the invisible guy resisted any urges to try a bite. He probably wouldn't have liked it any more than I did.

After dinner, none of us could find the TV remote, but I think I was the only one who suspected where it had gone. Along with my latest issue of *Spiderman*.

This was getting very irritating. Someone was stealing my life from all around me, and I couldn't do a thing about it. Naturally, my family didn't spot anything at all out of the ordinary. Not even when my cola glass disappeared from the coffee table while we were all watching TV.

I was getting madder by the minute. Pieces of my property were constantly disappearing into nothingness. I felt as though my life was being chipped away, piece by piece. It's a very disturbing feeling.

At bedtime I wasn't too surprised to discover that my toothbrush was gone. Luckily, I had a spare. As I climbed into bed, my socks levitated and disappeared.

"Knock it off," I grumbled. "It's time *you* were

in bed, too." Then I ignored him and went to sleep.

My paper route the next morning was free of interference again. Maybe the crook had stolen enough papers to make him happy. But I had to be on full alert the whole time I worked, of course, because I couldn't be sure he wouldn't change his mind as soon as I let down my guard. I was in a majorly bad mood.

School was—well—school. Even in Eerie, school is mostly boring, just like it was in Jersey. Science is always kind of interesting, though. I like to pay attention so I can find out what laws of nature are being routinely violated in Eerie. And today there were a few extra surprises in store for me.

Jazen was there, as always. He made a habit out of not volunteering to answer any questions, and kept a generally low profile. But Mr. Dupries didn't allow that to deter him.

He's one of those cheerful teachers who has made up his mind that everyone in class has to participate. He made a habit out of calling on people who didn't want to volunteer. Naturally, Jazen, being the quiet-as-a-clam type, had immediately drawn Mr. Dupries' full attention.

"Light is fascinating," he was saying. "It was once thought that light was infinite in speed, but we now know that this isn't the case. What's the speed of light in a vacuum, Jeni?"

Jennifer Grelski blinked back from her own private world and into this one. "Um . . . " she said brilliantly.

"No, it's a bit faster than that," Mr. Dupries said. "Jazen?"

"Two hundred eighty-two thousand miles per hour," Jazen replied. "Approximately."

"Faster than a speeding bullet," muttered Jeni.

"Correct," Mr. Dupries said. "And light is governed by the theory of relativity. Jazen, for bonus points, who formulated the theory of relativity?"

Even I knew that one: Albert Einstein. It didn't take an "Einstein" to know it. . . .

But Jazen looked totally confused.

After a moment, Mr. Dupries asked, "Jeni?"

"Duh. Albert Einstein," she replied, giving Jazen a smug look.

"Right." Mr. Dupries stared at Jazen. "Didn't your last school teach you about Einstein?" he asked.

Jazen looked embarrassed. "Uh . . . wasn't he

the guy who went to Africa and founded a hospital?" he asked desperately.

"That's Albert *Schweitzer*," Jeni said, rolling her eyes. "Like, what planet are you from?"

"That's enough, Jeni," said Mr. Dupries.

Jazen flushed. "I'm sorry, but ancient history isn't my specialty," he snapped back, obviously embarrassed and annoyed.

Ancient history? I stared at him. I knew we were talking turn of the century here, but a hundred years back isn't that ancient.

"Then perhaps you'd better do a little extra reading on the two Alberts tonight," Mr. Dupries suggested. Then he moved on to pick another victim. Unfortunately it was me.

"And whose experiment proved that the speed of light is a finite figure . . . Marshall?"

I had to think about that one for a minute. "Uh . . . Michelson-Morley," I finally answered. It was enough to get me off the hook for the rest of the period. But it made me wonder just what was wrong with Jazen. How had he messed up such an easy question so badly? And why had he used the word *ancient*? He was getting more and more mysterious every day.

And it got worse later that afternoon. We had

gym, which is okay. I never knock myself out, because that's a good way to get picked for teams I couldn't care less about joining, but I always do well enough so that I'm not the kid nobody wants on their team.

I was interested in seeing how Jazen did. If he was our thief, then he would have to have superhuman strength, and gym was just the place to spot it in action.

But he showed absolutely no superhuman prowess whatsoever. He tried the bench press, and handled even less weight than I did. I was watching him, and I'm pretty sure he wasn't faking it. There was real sweat on his forehead when he tried it, and his muscles were almost tied in knots. He was definitely weaker than me. And when we were doing pull-ups, he could barely do three.

He couldn't be the same guy who was the invisible thief. He'd never be able to pick me up, let alone Simon and me at the same time. So my main suspect had to be eliminated.

Except, there was nobody else in the class who seemed likely. It's possible our thief wasn't from my grade, of course, but he had looked about my age and size.

I was getting more and more confused about this whole thing. In fact, I was getting very depressed, until it started to rain. I looked outside the window during English, and saw the water falling from the sky, and my eyes just lit up.

I'd had an idea.

After school, Simon and I met up. Thankfully, the rain had stopped by now, but the grass was really soggy. It was just the weather for tracking mud all over the house, which my Mom had always told me not to do. But mud was just the thing I needed right now.

As soon as I was sure that Jazen was in earshot of us, I told Simon loudly: "I've got a bunch of old baseball cards that I don't need any more. Let's go over to the old building site and play hurling." Simon, naturally, agreed.

I'm sure you play "hurling," whatever you call it. It's when you take cards and see how far you can flick them. Whoever throws the farthest wins both his and the opponent's cards. It goes on until one person wins all the cards.

Simon and I didn't play it very often, but I wanted Jazen to know exactly where we were heading. If he was the thief, then he'd want to get there first and grab the cards.

Simon and I loitered a bit and grinned at each another as we watched Jazen hurry away to the site ahead of us. Then we followed after him.

Just as he'd done the previous day, he slipped into the Foreman site. And we went after him. This time, though, we had him trapped.

The yard was nothing but dirt—and dirt plus rain equals mud.

Simon and I looked down at the ground. There was a beautiful set of prints headed straight for the Porta-John. They didn't come out again.

"So he *did* go in there," Simon said quietly, his eyes sparkling. "Now what?"

"Now we take a peek," I told him. I was absolutely convinced we wouldn't see what we should see.

I tried the door, which opened easily. But when I swung it open, the little room was empty.

"That's crazy," Simon said, staring down at the mud. "The prints only go in. How could he have disappeared?"

"He didn't exactly disappear," I replied. "Look at the floor."

On the floor there were two muddy footprints leading toward the left side wall.

"I don't get it," Simon said. "He didn't go out

through the wall, did he?"

I checked outside in the mud. It was clear of footprints. "Nope." I shook my head. "He's got to be still in here somewhere."

"But he isn't," Simon pointed out.

"I know." I sighed. "There's something even weirder than normal happening here, and I don't know what. But if he *is* still in here, then he has to come out sometime. All we have to do is wait."

We closed the door again and retreated several yards. To pass the time, we halfheartedly hurled a few cards. Neither of us threw very far, but that's because we had more than half an eye on the Porta-John. We weren't looking directly at it, of course, but we could just see it out of the corners of our eyes.

After a few minutes, the door opened softly and then closed again. There was nothing there.

But several fresh footprints appeared in the mud and there was a soft squishing sound.

Jazen *was* the invisible thief, then!

Simon and I looked at one another and nodded.

Then we whirled around and jumped for the point where the footprints had stopped.

We both hit the invisible thief, and it was like running into a brick wall. I was dazed, but still managed to grab hold of an invisible arm. Simon did the same. If this was Jazen, he'd changed a lot. Not only was he invisible, but he was also back up to superhuman strength again.

He lifted Simon and me effortlessly into the air, whirled around, and then threw us both away as easily as if we were rag dolls. We barely had time to scream in panic before we landed in soggy heaps in the mud. By the time I recovered, I saw fresh tracks heading for the gate and the street.

"He's gone," I said. "He was too much for us again."

Simon looked down at himself. His clothes were covered with mud. "My mom's going to be furious," he said. "I'm filthy."

"At least the mud broke our landing, not our necks," I pointed out.

"My Mom'll break my neck," Simon complained.

We got to our feet, both looking like refugees from a mud wrestling competition. "We've lost him now," I said. "Out on the streets we'll never be able to track him. We were so close, too."

"He's got to know that we're on to him now," Simon pointed out. "So he's going to be doing whatever he can before we can expose him."

I saw Simon's point immediately. "More thefts. Back at my house."

"Right," Simon said, as we hurried for the gate.

"Where Dash is still setting up his trap," I finished. "And he told us to make sure that the thief stayed away until six." I glanced at my watch. It was barely four.

It looked as though we'd just lost our thief, in more ways than one.

5

"We've got to stop him," I said as we dashed out onto the street. Naturally, nothing was in sight, except for a couple of passersby. How could we stop Jazen from going to my house before Dash was ready for him? What might make him turn aside?

I grabbed the baseball cards from my pocket. "Jazen!" I yelled. "Baseball cards! Come and get them!" Then I hurled the first one toward the sidewalk ahead of me.

Simon shook his head. "He's got to realize it's a trick," he said sadly.

"Yeah," I agreed. "But it might still work, anyway. It all depends on how badly he wants my stuff. And considering the junk he's stolen already, I'll bet that these old trading cards are more than he can resist." I was carefully watching where the first one had fallen to the ground, and silently willing Jazen to come back for it.

I had no clue as to why he was so fascinated by my old stuff, but it acted on him like a flame does on a moth, or pollen on a bee. I was betting that he'd be unable to resist a freebie like this.

And I was right. After about fifteen seconds, the card suddenly rose up into the air and disappeared.

"We've got him," Simon said breathlessly, hardly daring to believe it.

"Never underestimate the power of greed," I told him. Then I held up the next one. "Here we go, Jazen," I said, and tossed it to the sidewalk just in front of me. Then I backed off, heading away from my house. Simon fell in with me.

Two local women were watching us with isn't-that-sweet expressions on their faces. "How adorable," the first one said. "They're playing with an imaginary friend."

"Aren't they a bit old for that, though?" said her companion.

That did it. I'm normally a calm sort of guy, but I hate being patronized when I'm fighting for my sanity. I dropped the third card right between them as I passed by, and held up the fourth.

I couldn't help grinning when my "imaginary friend" shoved the two startled women aside in order to grab the card. That served them right! They jumped back in surprise. Then, this being Eerie, they continued their previous conversation as if nothing out of the ordinary had happened. Maybe they were shoved around by invisible people every day. Who could know?

As Simon and I hurried away, we dropped cards at about half-block intervals. Each of them floated into the air a few seconds later and then disappeared, so we knew Jazen was still following us. All we had to do was to keep him busy . . . for the next two hours.

But I was running out of cards.

I only had three more left, and when they were gone, my hold over Jazen would be gone, too. He'd head back to my house for another stealing binge. What I needed was another idea, and fast.

Then I was down to the last card, which I held carefully. "Time to try reasoning," I said to Simon. We both stopped, and turned around. I held up the card so Jazen could see it. "Okay, Jazen," I said. "I know you're there, and I know that you're stealing my stuff for some reason. Why not drop the acting and just talk to me? I promise I won't be mad. I just want to know what all this is about."

There was absolutely no reply, but I was sure he was still there, eyeing the last card I held. What was he doing this for? I had to know. It was driving me crazy.

"Come on, Jazen," I begged. "I'll give you whatever you want, no strings attached. I just want to know why you're doing this. It's driving me nuts."

Still there was no reply. I was beginning to suspect that there never would be. Jazen didn't seem to be at all interested in dialogue.

"Now that I know it's you," I pointed out, "you can't come to school any more. Because for some reason you're visible and not super strong at school. So, come on—*please* tell me what this is all about."

I might have been talking to nobody, for all the response I was getting. Maybe I *was* talking to nobody. What if he'd decided that it wasn't worth waiting for the last card and had already left?

I tossed the last card. It disappeared in midair. Jazen was still there, all right. But he wouldn't stay for long, now that I had no cards left.

But the good news was that we weren't far from the World of Stuff. I turned to Simon. "How much money do you have?"

He shrugged. "A couple of dollars, I guess."

"Me, too. It might be enough." I looked at the

spot where the last card had disappeared, hoping Jazen hadn't fled immediately. "If you want some more cards, you'd better follow me," I said. "I'm going to get more right now. You can either come along or not. Suit yourself."

Simon and I started off for World of Stuff. Was Jazen following us? We couldn't hear or see anything, so there was absolutely no way to tell until we reached the store. We could only hope that he was sticking around for easy prey. Otherwise, whatever Dash was planning would go down the tubes.

We walked slowly, but not too slowly. We were trying to waste time, but not so obviously that Jazen would get bored and go away. It was getting close to five o'clock when we reached World of Stuff and went inside.

Had Jazen stuck with us, or had he given up?

The door opened behind us and closed. Nobody came in. Simon and I exchanged glances. We still had our fish on the hook. It was time to see how long we could play it.

Mr. Radford greeted us. "Hello, boys. What'll it be today? Malteds?"

"Trading cards," I told him, pulling out all the cash I had on me. Simon added his stash, and we had just five dollars and three cents between us. "How many packs will this buy us?"

"Depends on just what you're looking for," Mr. Radford replied. "I've got some fine new sets, just in." He showed us the boxes on the counter. "Brooklyn Dodgers, one of our best sellers for years. The Edsel collection, another classic great. The Ed Wood collection . . ." He went on at length about all the different sets he had in stock. In the end, we bought ten packs, one from each of ten different collections. The door hadn't opened by itself again, so Jazen was sticking with us, at least for now. We said good-bye to Mr. Radford and left the store.

I opened the first pack, a mint set of '57 rookie cards, and fanned them out in my hand. Eight cards, in bright colors. That meant we might have about eighty cards in all. If we couldn't keep Jazen busy for an hour with those, then we were done for. But I was willing to bet we could.

We went to the park and sat on one of the benches, looking for all the world like we were going to feed the ducks. Actually, in Eerie, there aren't any ducks in the pond. There are archaeopteryxes, which were supposed to have died out with the dinosaurs. We pretended to feed the birds, but instead we were tossing baseball cards.

Well, *I* was tossing them. Simon threw one of his at one point. Jazen ignored it until I picked it up and tossed it. Then he snatched it up.

"So it has to be mine," I realized. "It's not the cards you're after. It's the fact that they're cards I've handled. Why is that, Jazen?"

No reply. It didn't matter what we said to him, he refused to answer.

The hour dragged on, and by the time we opened the last pack, it was almost six. We'd stalled long enough, and managed to gain a few snippets of information. Now it was time for Dash to do his stuff.

I got up and opened the last pack. These were of song-and-dance film stars. Fred Astaire went flying first, followed half a block later by Gene Kelly. Jazen was on them immediately, snatching each one up.

"I just hope Dash has done his job," Simon hissed to me as we walked back slowly. "The suspense is killing me."

"I just hope that the trap doesn't hurt Jazen," I muttered back. "He's driving me crazy, but I don't want him hurt. I just want some answers." I let Rita Hayworth fly next.

It was after six when we finally arrived at the house and went around to the back.

Dash was on the deck, laid out in a chair with his feet on the table, apparently asleep.

"Uh-oh," said Simon, worried.

"Ditto," I added. We hurried over to Dash and shook him.

"Huh?" He opened his eyes and yawned. "Time to get started on the trap already?" he asked. "How long have I been sleeping?"

I couldn't believe it. All that time delaying, and the jerk hadn't done anything but sleep. "You idiot!" I yelled. "It's past six—the trap should have been set by now!"

"Past six?" Dash looked worried and glanced at his wrist. He didn't have a watch on. "Gee, guys, I'm sorry. All this planning's taken a real toll on me, I guess." He shrugged.

I felt like kicking him. We'd wasted our time and our last five dollars for nothing.

"We'd better get the basketball back, before 'Mr. Invisible' gets to it," Dash said, starting off the deck toward where the ball lay on the lawn. "Otherwise we'll have no bait for when I *do* set the trap."

But even as he spoke, there was motion on the lawn. The ball moved, then disappeared.

Actually, about three feet of the lawn

disappeared. There was a yell of surprise, and Dash let out his most evil chuckle.

"Boy, what a sucker," he gloated. "I knew he'd be expecting a trap, so I pretended I hadn't done it to make him overconfident, and it worked. I totally fooled him."

"You fooled me, too," I added.

Dash grinned. "I'm a pretty good actor when I want to be. Help me with this hose." He was unreeling the garden hose. "Simon, turn it on."

"What's all this for?" I asked him, confused.

"I dug a pit," Dash explained. "And then put the ball on a thin cover over it. Simple low-tech solution. When he went to pick up the ball, the cover gave way under his weight and dropped him into the pit."

"So why the hose?" I asked. Simon had turned on the faucet, and water was flowing.

"Because we have to force him to show himself, or else he might get out and past us again. This way, no matter how strong he is, he'll still have a slippery route out of here." We had reached the edge of the pit, and Dash played the hose down into it.

It was about seven feet deep and three across at the widest point. The water hit something invisible, and poured down over it. In the drops, I could make out a vague human shape.

"We can see you down there, now," Dash said loudly. "You won't be getting out of there without us stopping you." He grinned nastily. "I don't know how you manage this invisibility thing, but I'd love to learn."

There was already about four inches of water in the pit.

"We'll fill it up if you don't make yourself visible again. And I'm sure my two friends here will testify convincingly that I mean what I say," Dash added.

I was all too sure he meant exactly that. "We don't want to hurt him," I told Dash. "We just want to find out what's going on."

"He won't get hurt if he cooperates," Dash pointed out. "If he doesn't cooperate, then he deserves whatever he gets." He kept spraying Jazen down, and the water slowly rose.

Jazen tried to jump up twice. Each time, Simon and I pushed him back down. He might be super strong, but he couldn't get a firm hold on the muddy ground around the pit. Still he refused to give in or talk.

"He's tough, I'll give him that," Dash said,

when there was about eight inches of water in the hole. It was getting pretty muddy in there, too, so we could see two leg-shaped gaps in the muddy water where Jazen was standing. It was very weird. "Come on, kid, give it up. We've got a lot more time than you have."

Finally, Jazen realized that he'd been beaten. Dash had won honors again as the most devious person in Eerie. "Okay," Jazen said wearily. "You win. Turn off the water. I give up."

"Show yourself first," Dash insisted. "*Then* I turn off the water."

"Okay, okay." Jazen sounded totally dispirited, which was hardly surprising, considering how uncomfortable he had to feel. There was a slight buzzing sound, and then he was suddenly there, standing in the pit, absolutely soaked. He had his hand to his left wrist, where there was some kind of control device. It looked like a thick armband with controls on it. On his back he had what looked like an aluminum backpack.

"Okay, toss up the equipment first," Dash said, making no move to turn off the water. "I don't want you blinking out on us again."

Jazen sneezed, and did something to the wrist control. It opened up like a bracelet, and he slipped out of it. He threw it up and I caught it. It had several small buttons and a flickering screen that showed some sort of power levels, I guessed. It was like nothing I had ever seen before in my life.

Then he threw up the pack, which Simon caught. Despite the fact that it had to be made from some sort of metal, it seemed to be extremely light. Simon flicked open the top. Inside the pack were all the baseball cards. That's why they'd disappeared—once they entered the invisible pack, they'd become invisible also.

Simon dropped the pack on the grass, and then ran to turn off the water. Jazen looked terrible standing there, his hair and clothes absolutely drenched. Dash lowered the end of the hose into the pit.

"Grab hold," he growled. Jazen did, and Simon and I helped to haul him up. He staggered to his feet, dripping wet and looking totally miserable.

"Okay," I said to him. "Now let's have some answers."

Jazen shook his head. "You may have outwitted me," he replied. "But I'm not talking."

Great. We had the culprit, but still no answers. Now what?

6

"We'll see about that," Dash said, thumping his right fist into his left palm so hard that it made him wince. "I'll have you talking in fifteen minutes."

"No," I said firmly. "I told you, I don't want to hurt him."

Dash gave me a disgusted look. "Wimp. Look, we've caught him, so what do you want to do with him?"

"The first thing, I think," I replied, "is to get him some dry clothes. Otherwise he'll catch cold."

Dash rolled his eyes. "Please! Not only are you not going to rough him up a little, but you're going to play Mommy? Give me a break."

"Thanks for the help, Dash," I told him. "We can take it from here." I started to lead Jazen toward the house.

"Oh, no you don't," Dash said. "There was

something about splitting a reward, remember? I don't go until I get my share."

"Reward?" Jazen asked, puzzled. "What reward?" He sneezed. I was right, we had to get him dried off.

On our way upstairs to my room, I explained.

"I figured that if you were stealing from me, there had to be a reward out for you," I told Jazen. I hefted the bracelet. "After all, this is a pretty nifty theft device."

"I'm not a thief!" Jazen said, indignantly.

"Really?" I asked him. "You took my stuff without asking. That makes you a thief."

Jazen considered this for a moment. "Well, technically I guess it does," he was forced to admit. "But I never took anything valuable. Only small things. And you gave me the baseball cards."

"It doesn't matter how valuable the stuff was," Simon said. "Taking it without permission is stealing."

Jazen looked troubled. "Okay, I guess it is," he admitted. "But I couldn't just ask to take the stuff."

"Why not?" I wanted to know. I handed Jazen a towel. "Dry off while you're explaining."

He toweled his wet hair. "Because there are laws against such things."

"There are laws against stealing, too," Dash pointed out.

"That doesn't seem to stop *you*," Simon remarked.

"We're not talking about *me*," Dash growled. "We're talking about *him*."

I found some old clothes and handed them to Jazen. "You may as well wear these," I told him. "I'm sure you'd have stolen them soon, anyway."

"Thanks." He started to change out of his wet clothes.

I still wasn't buying his line. "So you couldn't ask for my stuff because there are laws against it?" I repeated, to make sure I had it right.

"That's right," Jazen said, pulling on the dry clothing.

"Laws where?" I demanded. "There are no laws like that here, not even in Eerie. So where do you come from?"

"Michigan," he replied promptly. "And that's all I'm allowed to tell you, so don't bother asking anything else."

I held up the bracelet. "As far as I know, they don't have anything like this in Michigan. Or in any other state, either. Where did you get it?"

Jazen shook his head. He was obviously taking his "laws" very seriously.

There wasn't much else I could do. I wasn't willing to let Dash rough him up. For one thing, I don't really believe in violence. For another, I kind of liked Jazen. True, he was strange, but so was almost everyone in Eerie. And he didn't seem like a bad kid. On the other hand, I still wanted some answers, and had to get them out of him somehow.

"Okay," I said, "let's go."

"Go where?" Dash demanded.

"The police station," I explained. "Jazen may not think he was stealing, but I think Sergeant Knight will have a different opinion about the matter."

That got through to Jazen. He looked startled, and then worried. "You can't turn me over to the police!" he exclaimed.

"I can and I will," I told him. "If you won't answer *our* questions, then maybe you'll answer *theirs*. Or just rot in jail for a few years."

He turned pale. "I can't go to jail!" he said. "I have to go home tomorrow night."

"Then I hope they have flights from the holding

cell," I answered. "Because that's where you're going to be." I gave him a big smile. "I guess there are laws against this, too, where you come from. But you're in Eerie now, and the laws are obviously different here. So, start talking or I'll have no choice but to call the authorities."

Dash scowled at me. "It doesn't look like there's going to be any reward for this kid," he complained. "Which means that you still owe me for my help."

Ouch. Dash wasn't one to forget a debt—as long as it was one owed to him and not the other way around. "So what do you want?" I asked him. "I don't have my allowance yet, or my paper route money."

"That's chicken feed." He sneered and pointed at Jazen's invisibility bracelet, which I was still holding. "I'll take that gadget in payment."

"That's mine," Jazen said firmly.

"And that stuff you took is Marshall's," he answered. "But that didn't bother you. This invisibility gadget might be yours technically, but it's going to be mine by possession." Dash held out his hand again. "Give it up," he demanded.

I shook my head. "Dash, I can see exactly what

70

you want to do with it. You'd use it for your own robberies, wouldn't you?"

"Dead right," he agreed. "I'll put it to much better use than stealing bubble gum and news-papers, though. I could walk into any bank in town and take whatever I wanted. Or any store."

"Then there's no way you're getting it," I told him. "I'm not going to help you start a crime wave."

"More like a crime tidal wave," Dash said happily. "Hand it over, or else I'll take it." He smiled nastily.

Unexpectedly, Jazen said: "You may as well give it to him."

"No way," I vowed. "I'm not letting him loose with this."

"It's okay," Jazen answered. "It won't work for him anyway. I shut it down. Until it gets the right password, it won't work again, for him, or you, or anyone." He folded his arms across his chest. "And it doesn't matter what you say, I won't tell you what the password is. There are laws against that sort of thing."

I winced. Why had I expected him to say that? Whatever was going on with Jazen, it was bigger and stranger than I'd first suspected. But Jazen's stubbornness had impressed Dash. He stopped trying to get the bracelet.

"So now what?" asked Simon, puzzled.

"We do what I said," I replied. "We take Jazen to the police. I don't care if it does mean he misses his flight home. He should have thought about that before he began stealing from me." I gave Jazen a shove toward the door. "Move it."

"Please," he begged. "Don't turn me over to the police. I'll be in so much trouble."

"So you have a record!" Simon breathed. He obviously thought we'd caught a criminal master-mind or something.

"Not trouble with the police," Jazen said urgent-ly. "They don't have any records for me at all. They couldn't have. I meant, when I get back home."

"In fifteen to twenty years," I told him callously. "Which is the time you'll be doing in prison."

Jazen was starting to get frantic now. "Marshall, you've got to let me go," he begged. "With the controller and the backpack. You've got to."

"I've already told you the terms for that," I answered, dangling the bracelet temptingly in front of his face. "You have to tell me what you're doing and why, and where you got this device. Otherwise, it's jail for you."

We were downstairs now. The patio doors were open, and I could hear Syndi in the backyard. "Marshall? Do you want some—" Then there was a startled gasp and a splash.

"Uh-oh," Simon said, getting pale. "We forgot to fill in the pit, didn't we?"

We definitely had. And now Syndi was in it, squealing with shock and rage. I was very tempted to just bolt for it and leave her down there, but I couldn't do that. She might catch a cold or worse, and it would be my fault. Reluctantly, we trooped out into the garden.

Syndi, not seeing the pit, had walked right into it. She stood in the bottom, glaring up at us as we circled the pit. "Marshall Teller, just wait till you see what I'm going to do to you!"

"Uh—you didn't find any tigers down there, did you?" I asked her, improvising like crazy.

"This is one of your stupid games!" she cried. "I'll bet you and your friends think it's very funny to trap me in a pit and soak me with water, don't you?"

Dash, naturally, couldn't resist stirring things up. "Well, actually, it is kind of funny," he admitted. Then he looked at me. "How about I hose her down a little?"

"No," I told him, as Syndi gave another yelp of anger. "I think we'd better help her out." I let down the hose again, and she grabbed hold. Simon and Jazen helped me to drag her out, while Dash just stood watching.

Syndi on dry land wasn't in any better mood than she had been in the muddy pit. She grabbed me by the arm. "I am going upstairs to change into clean clothing. And when I come down, you are going to be in hot water." She stormed off toward the house.

Simon jiggled my elbow. "Now might be a good time to run for it," he suggested.

"I think you're right," I agreed. I gave Jazen a gentle push. "It's time to book him."

As we hurried away from the impending Hurricane Syndi, Jazen tried again. "Marshall, I wish I could explain everything to you, but I'm not allowed to. I'll be in serious trouble if they find out I told you anything when I get back home."

"And you'll be in serious trouble right here if you don't talk," I pointed out to him. "It looks like a lose-lose scenario for you. So decide which you'd rather do."

We walked along in silence for a while. I could see that Jazen was thinking furiously, and it seemed best to let him make his mind up. I was sure that he'd come around to being reasonable in time. And I was right.

We were just a block from the police station when Jazen gave in. "All right," he said wearily. "I surrender. I'll explain everything. But you have to promise to keep this strictly to yourselves. If anyone ever finds out what I've done, I'll be in the worst trouble imaginable."

"Excellent," Dash said, as if this had been his idea all along. "So, let's hear some of the explanation. That bracelet, for example." He gestured at the control bracelet I was holding. "Where did you get it? And where can I get one like it?"

"I told you that part," Jazen answered. "You can get one of them in Michigan, where I live."

Dash shook his head. "Trust me, kid, they don't make things like that in Michigan."

"Not now they don't," he agreed. "But they do when I come from." At first I thought this was a slip of the tongue, and that he'd meant to say *where*. But it wasn't, and he hadn't. He stared at our vacant faces with some satisfaction. "I'm from Michigan, all right—but from the forty-second century."

7

"The forty-second century?" I echoed, astounded. Jazen, a time traveler?

Actually, it was starting to make some sort of sense. He *had* referred to Albert Einstein as "ancient history," and if he were from over two thousand years in the future, I guess it might well seem like that to him.

"That's right," Jazen agreed glumly. "I wasn't supposed to tell anyone at all about it, but you didn't give me any choice."

"Yeah, right." Dash sneered. "A likely story. Have you got any proof that you're from the future?"

Jazen indicated the bracelet that I still held. "That chameleon bracelet isn't a product of your time," he said simply.

I looked at it again. It did look like something from a science fiction movie, I had to admit. But it didn't look *that* sophisticated. "It doesn't seem like this is something that would take two thousand years to invent," I said.

"Actually, it isn't," Jazen admitted. "It's from the twenty-fourth century. You see, when we go back in time, we're supposed to only bring with us things that already existed in the time we're visiting. Just in case they fall into the hands of the locals. Which is exactly what's happened," he said, ashamed. "But I figured nobody would object to something so far out of your time, and it's so helpful when I want to collect things."

"It turns you invisible," Simon said, awed.

"Well, not exactly," Jazen explained. "It's a chameleon device. What it does is to make me look exactly like the background. This way you don't see me, you see what's beyond me. Kind of like the mythical animal, the chameleon, was said to behave."

"Mythical?" Simon said. "They're real. I once had one as a pet."

"Wow!" Jazen looked suitably impressed. "Then they must have died out between your time and mine."

"What else can this do?" I asked him, turning the bracelet over in my hand. "You seemed really strong when you were wearing it."

He nodded. "It's also like an exoskeleton. And it boosts my muscles, so I'm about five times as strong as normal. There's also a remote snatch device. That's what I used to grab the ball with yesterday."

"And the gum from my desk in class," I said.

"Right."

Dash's eyes were filled with greed. "I want that thing more than ever," he said.

"Forget it," I told him. "There's no way you're ever getting your hands on this. It would make you the biggest crook in the world."

"Exactly why I want it," Dash replied.

"I thought your main purpose in life was to discover who you are," Simon said, disgusted. "What's with wanting to become the next Jesse James?"

"If I'm stinking rich, I can hire other people to find out who I am for me," Dash pointed out. "Besides, if I've got to suffer from amnesia, I'd rather suffer in comfort, thank you very much."

I shook my head. "I'd give this back to Jazen before I let you have it," I told him.

"Actually, I was hoping you'd give it back to me anyway," Jazen said. "If I go back without it, I'll be in serious trouble. And so will you. The

Time Police would be forced to come back and get it, and you wouldn't like that any more than I'd like being imprisoned by your primitive police."

I didn't like the sound of that, but I had to admit it made sense. If he left something from three hundred years in my future in my hands, I might change the entire course of human history with it. "Maybe I'll give it back, then," I said. "I'll think about it."

"Don't be crazy, Marshall!" Dash said. "He's lying! There's no proof of his story yet. That device might be some secret weapon invented right here and now. It doesn't look that futuristic to me."

I considered his point, and realized that there could be some truth in what he said. Well, it can happen—even to Dash.

"He's right," I told Jazen. "This isn't really proof that you're a time traveler. We need more than this." It was possible—maybe not very likely, but possible—that Jazen had set up this whole thing as an alibi if he got caught. He might have been just pretending when he gave the wrong answers in school. I didn't know.

Jazen looked miserable. "The only way I can

prove it to you is to show you my time machine receiver," he finally said. "But there are laws against that. I'm not supposed to show primitives our technology." He flushed. "Uh, no offense."

"None taken," I assured him. I guess to a kid from the forty-second century, we would seem kind of primitive. Like, if I met a man from ancient Rome, or something. "But you've already broken a couple of laws, anyway. Would another one be all that much worse?"

He considered that. "I guess not," he said with a deep sigh. "After all, even if you told people, they wouldn't believe you, would they?"

"Going by my past experiences," I told him, "I think I could guarantee that without a problem."

Jazen made up his mind. "All right, then," he agreed. "But there's a couple of ground rules. First of all, you don't touch anything unless I tell you that you can. There's a lot of stuff in my capsule that could really hurt somebody who doesn't know what he's doing. And, second, you keep what I tell you to yourselves. Even if nobody would believe you, I don't want to run any risks. You can't imagine how much trouble I'd be in if my teachers knew I'd shown you my time machine."

"Okay," I said. "We promise."

"Yeah, sure," Dash said. But I could see the deceit in his eyes. "So let's get going already," he said. "The sooner you show us this machine of yours, the sooner we'll buy into your story."

Jazen nodded, and then headed east toward the building site, the rest of us following closely.

When we reached the gate, he paused. "I don't really have a Grandpa Foreman," he confessed to me. "I just borrowed the name from the gate here for school records."

"I kind of guessed," I told him.

We all followed him into the yard, and across to the Porta-John. Dash looked at it incredulously. "You travel through time in a toilet?" he jeered. "What do you do, sit on it and flush your way through time?"

Jazen looked annoyed. "It's another application of the chameleon bracelet technology," he explained. "It just *looks* like a toilet. Since I knew I'd be arriving at an abandoned building site, it seemed like the best disguise."

"Well, it certainly would have fooled me," said Dash. "And it's kind of small, isn't it?"

Jazen opened the door, revealing the interior you'd expect in a portable toilet. "It's transdimensional," he explained. "We can pack things up in subspace, and just leave a bit of them still sticking out into our universe. That way, we can carry all kinds of stuff with us in a small bag." He gestured at the pack, which Simon was carrying. "Like that bag. There's actually about half a ton of things in it."

Simon's eyebrows rose. "But it only feels like about ten pounds," he said.

"That's because the rest of the weight and mass is shunted off into subspace," Jazen continued. "You can't see it or feel it from the outside, but if you know the right trick, you can gain access to it from the inside. It's the same thing with my tent. It's in subspace, where it can't be found, unless you know the access point." He gestured at the far wall. "Which is here." He walked inside and then touched the wall.

Immediately a small control panel sprang into view. He tapped a small orange-lit control, and the entire wall opened up.

It was incredible. The opening where the wall had been now led into a corridor at least twenty feet long. But on the outside, it wasn't visible at all.

"Boy, this subspace thing sure helps conserve

space," Simon commented. "You can fit all that into one small Porta-John?"

Jazen shrugged. "We could fit an entire shopping mall in there if we wanted to. This is a pretty small shunt, with just my tent inside. Come on." He motioned for me to step into the corridor. Simon followed, and then Dash. Jazen closed the outside door behind us, and then stepped through into the subspace corridor.

Dash suddenly became very nervous. "Hey!" he snapped. "He's trapped us in here with him. Who knows what he's got in mind?" He looked as though he was going to punch Jazen.

The smaller boy held up his hands. "You're not trapped," he said quickly. "You can leave any time you like. You just have to tap the orange control, and the door will open. I only closed it so that if anyone comes into the building site for any reason, they won't see us in here."

That calmed Dash down, but he still looked uncomfortable, which was pretty much normal for him.

Jazen led the way down the featureless corridor and through the door at the end of it. "We have to have a bit of distance between space and subspace," he explained. "Otherwise there are problems. I'm not sure why, because I'm not very good at six-dimensional physics."

I'm not that good at plain old physics, so I couldn't criticize him. But I stopped in astonishment when we followed him through the door.

He'd called this his "tent," and I guess that was the right word for it—if the word for Buckingham Palace was the same as the word for house.

The tent was huge: at least sixty feet across and twenty feet tall. Off to the left was a small bed with a canopy. To the right was what looked like a kitchen area. Beyond that was a large wall screen, like a twenty-foot-tall TV. There were all kinds of gadgets and devices, including the weird bike I'd seen him riding when he stole my newspapers. It rested on the floor right now, though, instead of floating in the air.

"This is one cool place," Simon said in awe. "And it's just for you?"

"Oh, sure," Jazen said casually. "I call it my tent, but it's really my room at home."

"Your room at home?" This was getting stranger by the minute.

"Yes," he explained. "You see, in our time, rooms don't need to be fixed in one place. So, when they let me do this time transfer, I just had them move my room inside the tent. That way, I'd be the most comfortable."

"Wow," said Simon. "What a neat idea."

"I guess," agreed Jazen. He shrugged. "It *is* very convenient."

"I'll say," I agreed. "So, how about showing us around?"

Jazen looked as if he was going to refuse again, but then he shrugged. "Why not? You've seen this much, so I guess a little more won't do any extra damage." He led the way to the dining area. "Anyone want a snack?"

I hadn't eaten since lunch and was starving, but there didn't seem to be any cupboards or a place to cook food. "Sure," I said. Both Simon and Dash said the same.

Stepping over to the wall, Jazen touched it, and another control panel appeared. He tapped a couple of buttons, and there was a weird sort of popping noise. Then a bowl seemed to materialize out of thin air on the table. "Sit down and help yourself," he said, taking one of the chairs.

I shrugged and sat down. I looked at the bowl. It was filled with things I didn't recognize. I took one out and examined it. It was about the size and shape of a potato chip, but was slightly warm, and had a kind of chocolaty smell. It was also a pale green color. Maybe in his time that would be appetizing, but I'd seen more appealing food in mine. "What is it?" I asked.

"*Chuktar*," he answered. "It's from a planet about thirty light-years away from Earth, and it's my favorite snack." He took one and crunched down on it. "Try some."

Carefully I took a small bite and chewed it. The flavor exploded in my mouth, a sort of lemon creme chocolate, but like nothing I'd ever tasted before. I finished the first chip and grabbed a handful. Seeing that I hadn't been poisoned, Simon and Dash followed my example. For about ten minutes, we said nothing, all four of us content to eat until the bowl was empty.

"That was great!" Simon said. "I can see why it's your favorite."

Dash gave a loud belch and grinned. "Best thing I've eaten for as long as I can remember," he confessed. "In other words, about a year."

I looked around the tent enviously. "This is some place," I said admiringly.

"It's okay," Jazen said. "I keep trying to get my parents to update it, but you know how parents can be." He gestured at the wall screen. "I mean, three-

D is okay, but it's so *yesterday*. For me, that is."

"I can imagine," I said dryly. I made up my mind, and handed him back the chameleon bracelet. "I guess I have to believe your story now. There's no way all of this could be here if you weren't exactly what you said you were."

"Thanks, Marshall," Jazen said, placing the gadget back on his wrist but not activating it. "I really have been telling you the truth. But please, as soon as you leave here, try to forget everything you've seen."

"Okay," I agreed. "Simon, I think you can give him his backpack, too. You must be tired after carrying so much subspace around."

Simon did as I asked. "This is really neat," he said. Then he pointed to something at the other end of the table. "What's that?"

Jazen glanced at it. It was about six inches wide, and a foot long, with what looked like a keyboard and a screen on the top of it. "That's my Book o'Stuff," he answered. Seeing our puzzled looks, he explained. "It's like an encyclopedia would be in this day and age. I use it to look up anything I don't understand." He blushed. "I used it to check up on who Einstein was. I really did goof up in school today, didn't I?"

"Yeah," I agreed. "But you have a great excuse. I think this tent of yours would have given him nightmares if he'd ever seen it."

"You mean that book has anything you want to know in it?" Simon asked, impressed.

"Just about," said Jazen. "It's got more things in there than any two of your libraries would hold. It's how I knew where and when to find you, Marshall," he added.

"*I'm* in there?" I asked, astonished.

"I told you, just about everything is," Jazen said.

He'd answered almost all of my questions now. Except, of course, the one that I really wanted to know. "Okay," I said. "I accept that you're a kid from the forty-second century, no problem. What I still don't get is why you're here stealing my old junk. It just doesn't make sense to me."

"I guess it wouldn't," Jazen admitted. "Look, this is something I really shouldn't tell you."

Dash leaned forward. "Hey, you've broken so many rules," he said. "Why stop while you're on a winning streak? Go for one more."

After a moment's thought, Jazen nodded. "Okay. I guess I owe you that much at least." He took a deep breath. "It's because, in my time,

Marshall, you're known as one of the most important men of the whole twenty-first century. If not the millennium."

To say he'd stunned me would be a major understatement.

8

"Famous?" I gasped. "Me?"

Jazen nodded. "Definitely."

Dash grinned. "And I guess I'm even better known, right?"

Jazen looked at him, puzzled. "To be honest, I don't have the slightest idea who you are."

That wiped the smugness from Dash's face. "Dash Check," he said. "Though I might be known under my real name—if I knew what that was, of course."

Shaking his head, Jazen said, "Doesn't ring a bell. But, then, neither did Albert Einstein."

"I don't believe it," Dash muttered in disgust. "The nerd is famous, and I'm not. Where's the justice in that?"

I was still having trouble believing what Jazen had said. "What am I famous *for*?" I asked him.

"Sorry," Jazen answered. "I'm *really* not

allowed to tell you that. Let's just say that it's something you'll like, and leave it at that, okay? I'm not supposed to affect the normal flow of time, and if I give you any kind of information that might change your life, that's not all it might change."

"What do you mean?" I asked.

Jazen thought for a second. "Well, I'll give you a silly example. Let's say I knew that somebody was going to assassinate Mr. Dupries, your teacher. And then you prevented that murder from taking place. It would be nice for you and him, but it changes the course of history. It might be that his death would have inspired some person to achieve greatness, let's say. Or it may be that Mr. Dupries goes mad from teaching too long, grabs a gun and wastes half the class, killing some important people who should have done great things. The point is that changing anything in the past deliberately like that could cause chaos down the time lines. It's even possible that the world I know might cease to exist, and be replaced by something else. It's possible that *I* might not exist. After all, I'm the end product of a lot of marriages, and if just one of them didn't get to happen for some reason, then I wouldn't be born.

Somebody else would, maybe someone quite a lot like me. But it wouldn't be me. So, you see, I can't tell you any more. If I did, who knows what would happen?"

I could see the sense in what he was saying. Even though I was dying to find out what was in store for me, I could see that the price for that information would be way too high to pay. "Okay," I agreed reluctantly. "I guess I'll just have to wait and see what I do."

"That's the best thing," Jazen said.

"So," Simon interrupted, "I guess you can't fill me in on anything about my future either, huh?"

Jazen shook his head. "Sorry," he said. "But I don't think you'll be disappointed."

For a moment we were all silent, lost in thought.

Then Simon piped up again, "I still don't get why you're stealing all this junk from Marshall, even if he *is* going to become so famous."

"Oh." Jazen smiled. "It's the collectibles market. Everybody wants to have something that used to belong to Marshall. As you can imagine, not too many authentic relics survive from this age in the forty-second century. So I came back to get some." He tapped the backpack. "These baseball cards alone will make me a fortune."

"Couldn't you just have taken any old stuff back with you and claimed it was mine?" I asked.

"No," Jazen said. "For one thing, that's not honest. For another, each item's aura will be scanned to make certain that it was indeed handled by you. That's why I had to get authentic things you'd been using."

"A fortune?" Dash asked, fixated on the word.

"Yes," Jazen replied. "I can get very good prices for all of this stuff. It's a good job, really, because it'll take a lot to cover the cost of this time transfer. It's not cheap to go back twenty-two hundred years, you know. The fuel costs alone are enormous."

That had never occurred to me, but it made sense. It also explained why we weren't all tripping over time travelers every day. If it was so costly to make the trips, they'd hardly be very common.

"So," I asked him, "have you got everything you came for, then?"

"Very nearly," he answered. "I could do with some more pens, maybe some of your old school notes. Anything with your handwriting on it goes for a premium."

I couldn't help liking Jazen now that I knew

what he was up to. It was kind of flattering, to say the least. "I'll tell you what," I said. "Now that I know what you're after, why don't I just give it to you, instead of you having to steal it? This way, you can get to take your pick of whatever you like."

"Really?" Jazen's eyes lit up. "That would be cool. The only thing is that I have to make the transfer back tomorrow by six."

"This is a time machine," Simon protested. "Can't you just go whenever you feel like it?"

"No," Jazen replied. "It doesn't work like that. This is the receiver for a time machine. Sort of like your TV set is a receiver for broadcast signals from elsewhere. The actual machine is still back in my time. And it's set to take me home tomorrow at exactly six o'clock. So I have to be here by then, or the room will disappear without me."

"Oh." Simon looked concerned. "And then you'd be stuck here in the past?"

"No way." Jazen shook his head firmly. "That's *really* against the time laws. No, if I didn't go back, the Time Police would come after me. I'd be wanted, dead or alive. If I were to stay here, knowing what I know, I'd be bound to do something to muck up the time lines and change the future. If I missed the pickup, the police would either take me back and throw me in jail or kill me."

"Kill you?" Simon squeaked.

"Oh, yes." Jazen was very matter-of-fact about it. "Some sickos have tried to deliberately change the time lines in the past. The only way to stop them was to kill them. So, you can see that I really have to make it back as scheduled."

"Definitely!" I agreed. "But it gives us plenty of time. I'll find some of my old notes and stuff tonight, and if you come back home with me after school tomorrow, you can go through it and take whatever you want. And we'll have you back here in plenty of time for the pickup."

Jazen nodded, smiling. "Thanks, Marshall. That would be terrific."

I checked my watch. "Now, I really have to get going," I told him. "I've already missed dinner, and we've got a hole in my garden to fill in before anyone else thinks it's an in-ground pool."

"Okay." Jazen walked us back down the corridor and out of the Porta-John. "You know, I'm kind of glad that you found out about me, Marshall. It's been fun getting to know you all. This sort of thing almost never happens to me.

Except when I met George Washington, of course." He shook his head. "I wish I could tell you about that."

"But there are laws against it," I finished. "It sounds like there are more laws in your time than there are now."

"We've had over two thousand extra years to write them," he replied. "Why do you think we all need a Book o' Stuff?"

He had me there. We waved good-bye to him, and left the empty lot.

"Got to split, guys," Dash said immediately. "Things to do, places to see, and all that. I think I'll skip the 'Marshall Teller Admiration Society' meeting tomorrow. My stomach can only stand so much."

"Thanks for your help, Dash," I told him.

He smirked. "I'd say 'anytime,' except don't even think it. I've done my charity work for the year. Now it's time to look out for *numero uno* again." He walked off toward the woods. It's hard to know whether to like him or not. Sometimes he can be very helpful, and then sometimes he's just a real pain.

And he hadn't offered to help fill in the hole he'd dug, either.

The rest of the evening went as well as could be imagined. Simon and I got yelled at by my folks for digging a hole in the garden. We hadn't known that was what Dash was going to do, of course, but we could hardly use that as an excuse with my folks. Naturally, the two of us had to fill it in again.

Syndi was still angry with us, but not enough to avoid talking to us. She let us know just what she thought of reckless idiots who dug holes for her to fall into. I did feel sort of bad about what happened, so I couldn't blame her.

Then Simon went home, and I went inside. As punishment for digging dangerous holes, I wasn't allowed to watch TV for the evening, but that was okay. I had to go through my old notes, anyway. I dug out a lot of stuff from the back of my closet that I'd forgotten about, including old school papers and homework I could do without. It's amazing, the amount of junk you can accumulate without even trying. I decided to look on this as late spring cleaning.

And after all that work I really slept well.

The next morning, Simon and I met up with Jazen on the way to school. He'd loosened up a whole lot now that we knew his secret, and he was an okay guy to hang around with. At lunch, I gave him my straw and a plastic spoon, which went into his collection.

But in the afternoon, disaster struck.

Like I've already said, Jazen wasn't the most muscular guy in the world. But it's too bad you can't get excused from gym for that. In the middle of a pretty rough game of dodgeball, Jazen got hit and went flying.

When he tried to get up, he yelped in agony. I hurried over to help him, and he grimaced. "It's my ankle," he said, gritting his teeth. "It feels like I've broken it. I landed kind of hard."

Mr. Burgess, the gym teacher, was glaring down at him. "School nurse," he said.

"I'll take him," I volunteered. Jazen managed to stand on his uninjured foot, and I supported him as we set off for the nurse's office. "You okay?" I asked him. He looked kind of pale.

"I'm just worried about the barbaric rituals I'm going to have to undergo," he confessed. "No offense, but your medical technology is really primitive. In my time, this would be healed in minutes."

"It's a good thing you're going home later today, then," I pointed out. "But we're not that barbaric, you know. Doctors stopped using leeches ages ago."

"They did?" Jazen looked relieved. "Well, that's one worry off my mind."

I realized that he sometimes had as little idea of what went on in our time as I had about daily life in ancient Rome, and for pretty much the same reason.

The nurse didn't take long in examining his ankle. "I think it's just a sprain," she announced. "Nothing seems to be broken, but you should see your doctor." She put some cream on the ankle, then bound it with bandages. From the look of relief on Jazen's face, he must have been expecting her to decide to amputate it. "You'll need to give it some serious rest. No moon-walking for a while."

"Oh, I never walk on the moon," Jazen replied seriously. "Mars is much nicer."

Luckily, the nurse thought he was joking and just laughed. "Nice to see your sense of humor hasn't been sprained. Well, I think you'd better go home and stay off that foot. I can lend you a wheelchair as long as I get it back tomorrow. Should I call your parents to come pick you up?"

"Uh, I can see him home," I volunteered. "This is last period, after all."

With Jazen in the wheelchair, we headed back to the gym to change and tell Mr. Burgess where we were going. In fact, I pushed him over to our house first. His eyes lit up when he saw the pile of stuff I'd found for him. He quickly loaded it into his subspace bag, and then we were off to the building site. We still had plenty of time before Jazen was due to return home.

It took a little struggling for him to get into the port-a-john, since we couldn't fit the wheelchair in through the door. I helped him down the corridor and into his room. He collapsed onto the bed, sighing with relief.

"How's it feel?" I asked him.

"It's been better," he confessed. "But when I get home tonight, it'll be fixed in a couple of minutes. I guess I can endure it till then." He smiled at me. "Thanks for everything, Marshall."

"No problem," I replied. "Can I get you anything? Something to eat or drink? Something to read?"

"No, I'm fine, honest," he replied. "This bed can get me anything I like, in fact. And my Book o'Stuff is just . . . " His voice trailed off, and he stared with a frown at the small table next to the bed. There was a bottle of water there, but nothing else. "That's odd. I'm sure I left it there."

"Maybe you moved it," I suggested.

"I don't think so," Jazen replied. He reached over to a small control panel in the head of the bed and pressed a button. "Computer, locate my copy of the Book o'Stuff."

"The book is not within my scanning range," the computer replied, in a pleasant female voice.

"That's not possible," Jazen muttered, confused.

"What does it mean?" I asked him. "What's the computer's scanning range?"

"About half a mile," he replied grimly. "And that means the book isn't here, but that's not possible, is it?"

"You didn't take it anywhere, did you?"

He snorted. "You've heard me quoting the laws often enough. There's no way I'd take that book out of here. If it fell into the wrong hands, it could cause a disaster."

And then I knew exactly what must have happened to it. "Too late," I told him. "I think it already has. I'd bet anything that Dash has it."

Jazen went pale. "But . . . that could mean the end of my world!"

9

*T*his was bad news. "We have to get the Book o'Stuff back," I said firmly. "Before Dash can figure out how to use it. Do you think he's had time to read it yet?"

"I'm not sure." Jazen tapped the computer button again. "Computer, did anyone enter my room after I left for school this morning?"

"Yes, sir," the computer answered politely. "The individual who accompanied you home yesterday, noted in my memory banks as a Mr. Check."

"It was Dash all right," I grunted.

"When was he here?" Jazen asked.

"Fifty-three minutes ago," the computer replied.

"Less than an hour." Jazen was starting to look a little less shocked. "I don't think that's long enough for him to have worked out how to read the book. If we can get it back *now*." He started to rise from the bed, and then collapsed, wincing in pain.

"I'll have to get it back for you," I told him firmly. "You stay here and rest."

"But he's bigger and stronger than you," Jazen argued.

"Then I'll just have to outsmart him," I replied. I remembered what Jazen had said about the things that might happen if someone knew the future. I couldn't let Dash change the whole history of the world, especially if it meant that Jazen would stop existing. He'd become a friend, and I didn't want him wiped out.

"There's another possibility," Jazen said. "Over on the table there is the chameleon bracelet. Bring it over here. I want to show you something."

I handed it to him. He tapped in a code, and then held it out to me. "Use this," he said. "This way, you'll be stronger. And you can sneak up on him without being seen."

This was awesome. I couldn't believe how lucky I was. Not only was I going to be one of the most famous people of my time, but I was going to get to walk around invisible. I slipped on the bracelet, which fit as though it had been made for me. "Cool," I said. "What do I do?"

"Tap this blue button here to power up the bracelet," he told me. "The orange one underneath it switches it off again." He looked nervous. "Be careful, Marshall. We only have two hours until I have to go home. And if I go home without the book, then the Time Police will come for it. And nobody will enjoy that." He grimaced. "That's assuming I can go home. If Dash changes the future, it may not be there to go back to. I might end up being stuck here, after all."

"Then I'll get the book back before there's any harm done," I promised. "Wish me luck." I ran to the door, down the corridor, and out into the building site. There I almost ran down Simon.

"Hi, Marshall," he said. "I heard about Jazen's accident. Is he okay?"

"He may not be," I replied, and filled him in on what had happened as we half walked and half ran toward the woods. "So we have to find Dash before he can read the book," I told him. "Otherwise, the whole future might come crashing down around us."

Simon shuddered. "I can't think about it," he said. "But, Marshall—we don't know where Dash hides out."

"I know." It had occurred to me, too, but I

couldn't allow it to stop me. "We'll just have to go to where we ran into him the other day and start searching from there. He's got to live around there somewhere. Maybe there will be some sort of trail."

Simon nodded. "Too bad I never took my path-finder course in Cub Scouts," he said. "And you're not the best tracker in the world."

"Today we'll both have to be," I replied.

We reached the spot in the woods by four-thirty. That meant we had about an hour to find the shack and recover the book before we had to head back. Was it enough time? It would have to be.

I examined the ground in every direction from the spot where Dash had stood, and didn't have a clue as to which way he might have gone. Not from the direction we'd come, obviously. But that left plenty of other choices.

"We'd better split up," I told Simon. "You go left, and I'll go right. Ten minutes out, and then back again, whether you find anything or not. If neither of us does, we'll try the other directions."

Simon nodded, and set off. I went in the opposite direction as fast as I could. It wasn't easy, because these woods had been left wild. There were brambles, fallen branches and trees, and very uneven ground. After ten minutes, I was back. Simon met me a moment later, but neither of us had had any luck. So we tried again. And then again.

An hour later there was still no sign of Dash's shack. I was starting to feel sick, knowing that we didn't have time to get back to Jazen now, even if we did recover the book. But I wasn't going to give up.

And then I spotted it. It was an old building, definitely worse for wear and weather, but it had to be the right place. I tapped the button to activate the chameleon device. Nothing seemed to happen, though. Was it broken? If it was, then it wouldn't be of any use when I had to face up to Dash.

I went back to the clearing, where Simon was waiting for me. He was looking all around.

"I've found it, Simon," I told him.

Simon almost jumped out of his skin. "Marshall? Where are you?"

"Right in front of you," I told him. "Jazen gave me his chameleon bracelet. I guess it really works, then."

"Does it ever!" Simon exclaimed. "You're totally invisible."

It didn't look that way to me, but I realized it made sense. I was inside the field of the device, so everything looked normal to me. It was only if you were outside looking in that the chameleon field worked.

"Right," I told him. "You start back toward the building site. I'll grab the book and come after you. Just remember that Dash is likely to be right behind us and pretty mad."

"Okay. Good luck, Marshall." Simon waved at a spot about three feet from me, and then left.

I went back to the cabin, hoping that I was still in time. At least, now I knew I was invisible and super strong, even though I didn't feel like I was either. I hurried up to the shack, ducked over double until I realized that this was silly—Dash couldn't see me, anyway. I went to the window and peered in.

The place was a mess. Dash had scrounged up, salvaged, or stolen several bits of furniture, including the rickety old table where he was sitting. The book was in front of him, and he was tapping at the keys.

"Come on, come on," he muttered. "This has to work. I'm really wasting my time otherwise."

I felt a wave of relief. He hadn't managed to

access any information yet. There was still time to save the future!

And then I heard the computer voice say, "Access accepted. Please key in the entry you wish to find."

There really wasn't any time to be subtle. Dash had already started to type in whatever it was he wanted to check on first, chuckling happily to himself. It was time to act.

I kicked in the door and leaped across the room. Unfortunately, I had forgotten that the chameleon bracelet also gave me super strength. When I leaped, I overshot my target and slammed into the far wall of the shack with so much force I almost went through it.

Dash jumped, too, snatching up the book. "You're not getting it back, Jazen!" he yelled, and dashed out of the door.

I picked myself up off the floor where I'd fallen. I felt like a walking bruise. I could have really used it if the bracelet had made me invulnerable, too, but it hadn't. I'd really blown it. But I couldn't waste time in blaming myself. Instead, I chased after Dash.

Dash was bigger than me, but he wasn't really in shape. He was too lazy to exercise. And he was too panicked to try to hide. Instead he was running as fast as he could through the woods. I followed him, gaining bit by bit.

Finally, I was close enough to jump him again. This time, I was a lot more careful, and I managed to tackle him around the knees. With a cry, he fell down and rolled over. I grabbed the Book o'Stuff and pulled it from his hands.

"No!" he yelled. "Jazen, give it back!" He snatched at the air, trying to grab hold of me. But I jumped quietly to my feet and backed off as silently as I could. Naturally, he saw the book move in the air, and leaped up after it. "I've got to have it!" he yelled. "I want to find out who I am! I wasn't going to use the book to find out anything else, honest!"

I glanced down at it. On the screen, I saw that he'd typed: "Who were the winners at" before I'd stopped him.

Looking up who he was! As if. He was trying to get rich first by betting on some athletic event. And that could be enough to cause serious problems for Jazen.

I slid the book inside my jacket, and that must have made it go invisible, because Dash started to look all around where I was walking.

"Jazen," he begged. "Let's cut a deal. We can share all the money I make. I can put it into a bank. Just think how much interest you'd get in two thousand years! Come on, I know you're a businessman. Let's cut a deal."

I hurried away. Let him think it was Jazen who'd taken back the book. That way, I'd be off the hook, and he wouldn't be after me for it later. After all, I would have to live with Dash, like it or not, while Jazen would be . . . in Michigan.

The problem was, it was now ten minutes to six. There was no way I could get back to the building site in time with the book, which meant that Jazen would go back to his time without it, and then the Time Police would come after the book—and me.

The way Jazen had talked about them, they sounded like pretty tough characters. And they had a shoot-to-kill policy, which didn't exactly endear them to me.

On the other hand, what could I do about it? I was hurrying as fast as I could, but there was no way I'd make it back to the building site in time.

I was back on the main path then, and running full tilt, still invisible. If anyone got in my way, they'd be knocked down by an invisible hurricane.

I didn't have any time to be polite.

And then I stopped dead.

Zipping toward me was Jazen on his flying bike, with Simon hanging on for dear life.

"Jazen!" I yelled, forgetting for a second that I couldn't be seen. Then I tapped the off switch, and waved.

Jazen pulled up a moment later. "Did you get it?" he asked, desperately.

I handed it to him. "Is there still time?"

"On this, yes. Hop on, fast."

I did, and Jazen gunned the bike's silent motor, whirling around and heading back to the building site. I glanced at my watch. Four minutes to six.

That bike was something else. We flashed along, four feet from the ground. We had to be doing almost eighty miles an hour. The ground just slipped past us.

"I realized you'd run into trouble, so I came looking for you," Jazen called back to me over Simon's head. "I was praying you'd get the book back. You didn't try reading it, did you?"

"No," I assured him. "And Dash didn't get a chance to, either."

"Thank you so much, Marshall," he said sincerely. "You saved my life. Maybe literally. If

Dash had changed the flow of time . . ." He didn't have to finish that thought.

We zipped in through the gate of the building site with ninety seconds to spare. The wheelchair was still parked next to the Porta-John where Jazen had left it. He brought the bike to a halt, and as Simon and I tumbled off, he grabbed the book and hopped over to his time machine on his good foot and opened the door.

"Have a safe trip home," Simon called, pushing the bike in after Jazen.

With his sore ankle, Jazen could barely hold up the heavy bike. But finally he managed to tap the panel to get into the corridor.

"Bye, guys," he called. "It's been fun. Thanks for everything."

"No problem," I replied, waving back.

There was a whir of machinery, and Jazen grinned at us. "That's the activation. I'll be gone in a few seconds."

And then I realized I was still wearing the chameleon bracelet. If that didn't go with Jazen, then the Time Police would come for it. "Jazen, hang on!" I yelled, snatching the thing from my wrist. I tossed it through the still-open door.

It landed with a splash.

Then the Porta-John shivered as though it was in its own private earthquake. Simon and I stepped back a couple of paces, and watched it shudder. It became blurry, like a picture going out of focus. And finally, it just popped out of existence. There was a swirl of air rushing into the place where it had stood, and then nothing.

EPILOGUE

Simon and I walked toward home. For a few moments neither one of us spoke. Then Simon turned to me. "Wow," he said. "That was some show."

"Yeah," I agreed, relieved that everything had turned out okay. "I just hope Jazen doesn't get into trouble if they have to fish that bracelet out of the john, though."

Simon laughed. "At least they've got everything."

"Yeah. And Jazen's got plenty of collectibles to sell." I shook my head. "It's really weird, thinking that in two thousand years people are going to go crazy to buy my old baseball cards and ballpoint pens, though."

Simon nodded. "But isn't it great, knowing you're going to grow up to be somebody really famous?"

"It sure is," I agreed. "It's also scary. Now I know I've got to do something with my life. It was bad enough before, when my folks just kept telling me I should do something. Now I know they're right, and it worries me. What if I don't manage?"

"You've got to manage," Simon answered. "The history books of the future say you do." He grinned. "And I knew you before you were famous."

"So you did," I told him. I started to push the wheelchair back toward the gate. "Hey, you know, we never got the details about your life from Jazen."

"My life?" Simon laughed. "I'll be lucky just to grow up. I'm not going to be famous." He offered me a stick of gum, and then took one for himself. Then he tossed the wrapper away.

"Simon!" I scolded him. "You should throw that in the trash can."

"Oops, sorry," he said. He went to pick it up.

But the wrapper had disappeared.

We looked at each other. "You don't think . . . ?" he asked, worried.

"No," I answered, not entirely convinced. "It can't be happening all over again . . . can it?"

THINGS CAN'T GET ANY EERIER, OR CAN THEY?

Here's a sneak preview of
the next Eerie adventure,
Eerie Indiana #5: Fountain of Weird,
Published by
Macmillan Children's Books

*O*utside, the morning had an icy chill and wind whipped up trash in the street. Weird. It should've been hot and muggy, like a normal summer day. Then I caught myself. Normal? Ha! Nothing is normal in Eerie, Indiana.

We jumped on our bikes and took a shortcut through downtown to the landfill. Mr. Periwig was taping a sign to the window of his barber shop.

WEDNESDAY: HAIRCUTS HALF PRICE.

BRING YOUR OWN BOWL.

I considered it. My hair had been getting a bit shaggy lately.

Eerie's landfill was the perfect spot for the annual

swap meet. The crater was larger than Kratatau. That's east of Java. Anything that couldn't be sold would be buried under a ton of dirt. Since it was already in the landfill, it would be easy.

Simon and I zipped by the traffic on our way there. I pedaled into a cold wind and sucked in a lungful of freezing air. For a second I thought I smelled formaldehyde, an odor I recognized from science class. I filed the information in my brain under "weird." Maybe I'd have time to investigate the smell later.

After a few miles the asphalt highway gave way to a rutted dirt road. Secretly I hoped to discover our missing walkie-talkies at the swap meet in someone's junk. Things have a way of turning up in unexpected places here in Eerie.

Soon the dirt road was jammed with station wagons, minivans, and a school bus filled with retirees from the senior center. Horns honked and tempers flared as vehicles tried to inch their way to the dump, everyone wanting first dibs on the junk.

Simon and I stopped at the top of the landfill to catch our breath. An old lady sped by us on a unicycle. "Go for the burn!" she cried, her words riding the dust kicked up from her tire.

We looked at the landfill. It was a huge crater

and there were rows of booths set up inside it. The booths were surrounded by twisted car frames and piles of disposable diapers that had been lying out there for years.

Off to one side, the entertainment was rehearsing. A band from the Texas Mosquito Festival was tuning up.

There was also a cluster of circus acts waiting to perform in the center of the landfill. A slender woman from the circus slipped a banner over her shoulders. It read CAUTION: WIDE LOAD.

"The circus must not be doing so hot these days," said Simon. "The fat lady couldn't weigh more than 99 pounds."

We pushed off down the steep road that eventually wound around to the landfill.

When my dad and I had been here earlier I'd picked a spot as far away as possible from my parents' booth. It didn't seem right to be competing with them. Besides, I didn't want to be near my sister, who was dressed like a garbage can.

Simon was unloading his wagon when a friend from school strolled over.

"What're you guys selling?" Sara asked, a stack of dog-eared paperbacks in her arms.

I found myself staring at her backpack, wondering

if a pair of walkie-talkies was inside. *Stop it!* I told myself. This was Sara I was thinking about, winner of the Battle-of-the-Books (B.O.B.) competition.

The entire Lee family were bookworms, especially Sara's mom, Mrs. Lee, who devoured cookbooks, recipe by recipe. She owned Eerie's bakery, Sweet Tooth.

Sarah had inherited a taste for literature, reading everything from Laura Ingalls Wilder and Mary Wollstonecraft Shelley to Martha Stewart and Betty Crocker.

"Just a bunch of junk," I finally said. I didn't want her spending her money here. I knew she was trying to save for the B.O.B. finals next month in Washington, D.C.

Sara opened one of her paperbacks. "What's the difference between dandruff and nose hair?" she asked.

"Beats me," I said.

Simon thought for a moment. "Nothing," he said. "They're both gross."

"That's right Simon!" She beamed at him. "Have you read this book?"

Simon shrugged. "I don't think so."

Sara started picking through our junk.

I could tell there wasn't anything she really

liked. She just wanted to hang out with Simon. She'd had a crush on him for a few weeks, although Simon would never admit it.

Finally Sara walked toward the food booth run by Sir Lancelot. All the sausages you could spear for $2.95.

"See ya later," she said.

I nudged Simon. "Love is like the common cold. You never know when you're going to catch it."

Simon blushed, his freckles matching his hair. "Not if I live a thousand years!"

Sara Lee's mom, I noticed, shared a booth with Harriet Nelson. They were selling baked goods: fudge, cakes, cookies shaped like rock stars. The Grateful Dead were the most popular cookies because the whole band was sprinkled with nuts.

So far the swap meet seemed normal enough—at least by Eerie's standards. But I knew from experience to expect the unexpected. Being prepared wasn't everything in Eerie. It was the *only* thing.

Looking back on the day's events, I realize I should have paid more attention to certain clues. Namely, the smell of formaldehyde. Still, how could I have known a mad scientist was lurking in our midst?

A selected list of titles available from Macmillan and Pan Books

The prices shown below are correct at the time of going to press. However, Macmillan Publishers reserve the right to show new retail prices on covers which may differ from those previously advertised.
